California Odyssey

by Jack Frakes

Baker's Plays
7611 Sunset Blvd.
Los Angeles, CA 90042
BAKERSPLAYS.COM

CHARACTERS

MALE
- **CORKY SAYLORS**
- **TAD MILLER**
- **MALE CARNIE: BARKER**
- **HERMAN**
- **RELIGIOUS PERSON**
- **E.L. "SPIT" PARTCH**
- **VILLAIN**
- **STORMY O'BRIEN**

FEMALE
- **JINX O'BRIEN**
- **WOMAN CARNIE #1**
- **WOMAN CARNIE #2**
- **LITA**
- **ZULIE**
- **MARGO LOVEJOY**
- **ROSIE**
- **BEVERLY "BABE" BORDEN**
- **SALLY**

Because of the episodic nature of the play there are many creatively different ways to cast that could give maximum involvement and experience for many actors. When a character appears only once in the story, he or she could easily appear later in another role with a different make-up, costume, voice and character qualities. (See the "Production Notes on Casting" in the back of this script for many casting possibilities.)

PLACES / SETTINGS

There are different locations in California that include two or three playing areas, depending the size of the stage. The "Car," is where most of the scenes take place, is at stage right or center. The other one or two areas involve simple settings for: Carnival Concession, Swan Café, Mobile Home, Desert Oasis Gas Station and Street Scene in San Diego's Gaslight District that includes the whole stage. Signs, furniture and props define the specific location. The areas may overlap, particularly if the stage is small. (See Production Notes for details.)

TIME

Present day. Early June. All the action takes place from Friday night till Sunday noon.

CHARACTER DESCRIPTIONS
(In Order of Appearance)

CORKY SAYLORS

In his 20s. He is blond. He is a breezy, optimistic, friendly, and slightly zany beach bum, with a free and mischievous spirit. He is a photographer who takes pictures of everything. He is also cousin and friend of Tad's. Wears bright clothes of yellow, blue and green, casual floppy tennis hat, sailor-like clothes.

TAD MILLER

In his 20s. He has dark hair. He is a serious, overly organized, practical, and pessimistic desert rat. Wears dark clothes of brown, burnt orange and black. Wears Levis or cords, and western Texas hat with plaid or checked shirt and possibly a vest.

JINX O'BRIEN

In her 20s. She has reddish hair in a pageboy. She is charmingly flirtatious, curious, trusting, intense, somewhat wild, and yet vulnerable. At times, she has a child-like innocence, and at other times she is sensitive and seductive. She wears necklace and rings and colorfully accented scarves of pinks, reddish-orange and jade green. Her clothes should be a bit outlandish, but appropriate – and not really "tacky" or overdone.

THREE CARNIVAL WORKERS:

Male Carnie: Barker, Woman Carnie # 1, Woman Carnie # 2

They could be almost any age, from 30s to 50s but are most likely in their 40s. They should have a quality of charming earthiness about them, although they are a little suspicious and cynical about outsiders. They can be dressed colorfully – possibly in stripes and checks and plaids, which clash. Vests, money aprons and possibly a straw hat on the Male Carnie: Barker, and maybe a derby or baseball cap on Women Carnies #1 and #2. Or, the women could just have hair piled high. They probably wear something like tennis shoes for comfort.

UNCLE HERMAN

In his late 40s to late 50s. Husband of Lita. Owner and operator of the Silver Spur General Store and Post Office outside of King City. A big, burly bear of a man who is kind and friendly. Admires Stormy.

AUNT LITA

Wife of Herman. She's in her 40s. She's a waitress and owner of the Swan Cafe outside King City. A healthy, hearty, loud, rough-hewn, but warm woman. An old but good friend of Stormy's. Now feels confined to the Swan Cafe. Probably wears waitress outfit and has a pile of hair on her head.

ZULIE

Lita's daughter is a spunky 13 year-old with freckles. She could have red hair with pigtails.

MARGO LOVEJOY

In her 50s. Jinx's mother, who lives in a Santa Monica in the Elysian Fields Mobile Home Park. Can't stand Stormy's lifestyle. Likes to think of herself as a great actress, but is currently a fortune-teller and drama teacher, who works in a run down movie theatre. Always a little harried, grand in style and movie struck.

ROSIE

In her 50s. A plain little mousy friend of Margo's, who has read a lot of Shakespeare and speaks with precise diction.

RELIGIOUS PERSON

Could be male or female. Probably male of indeterminate age. Sanctimonious: appearing to be or sounding holy and pious, but hypocritically holy. Is well-kept, clean and neat. Makes phony, pious gestures: smiles sweetly, and insipidly.

E.L. "SPIT" PARTCH

Late 60s or older. An old prospector who's a friend of Stormy's. He spits and scratches a lot. Has a shaggy, droopy mustache and possibly a scraggly beard. He wears dirty, weather-beaten cowboy or work clothes with a hat that has a turned-up safety-pinned brim in front. Carries a gun, canteen, possibly back-pack, etc. He's a crusty, cagey old codger.

BEVERLY "BABE" BORDEN

Sam age as Tad...mid to late 20s. Owner of Desert Oasis Gas Station near the Salton Sea. She's an old girlfriend of Tad's. But she's changed from an innocent, awkward gauche young girl that Tad described to her present warm, hearty, saucy, bouncy, no-nonsense, self-confident young woman who's ready to leave her rural environment and go tackle the world.

VILLAIN

A stereotypical villain who appears at the end of the play in the film that is being made in the Gaslight District in San Diego.

SALLY

Tad's sister who is getting married. She is in her early 30s, bright, alert, and vibrant, but somewhat erratic and erotic and full of life.

STORMY O'BRIEN

Late 40s to early 50s. A hearty, muscular, charming, lovable, exasperating, out-going old style cowboy with a devilish sense of humor. He has red hair and wears a cowboy hat.

ACT I

(Sausalito, California, a town just across the Golden Gate Bridge from San Francisco. In the kitchen of a house near the waterfront. It is about 10:30 on a Friday night. **CORKY SAYLORS** *is in a single spotlight. He is talking to someone on the phone in a secretive whispering tone. As he talks he glances offstage, not wanting to be heard.)*

CORKY. Hi, This is Corky. We're all set up here, and we're leaving around seven in the morning. How are things going down there?

(Beat. Offstage, a cough. **CORKY** *glances off.)*

Uh-huh, uh-huh, Oh, yeah. I understand why that's embarrassing, and you don't want to do it.

TAD. *(off)* Who are you talking to?

CORKY. Okay then, I'll do everything I can to make us as late as possible. *(beat)* No, no, it's your wedding and Tad doesn't need to know. I won't tell him a thing.

TAD. *(off)* Hey, Corky! Who's that on the phone?

CORKY. Oh, sure. I'll make sure we go that way. We'll be on Highway 17 about 8:30. I'll watch for her near the Summit.

TAD. *(off)* Corky! Who is it?

CORKY. Gotta go. See you whenever we get there…sometime on Sunday. Meantime, good luck.

(He hangs up just as **TAD MILLER** *enters from offstage.* **CORKY** *looks slightly sheepish and guilty.)*

TAD. *(yawning sleepily)* Who're you talking to at this time of night?

CORKY. Nobody.

TAD. What did nobody want?

CORKY. Nothing.

TAD. What were you talking about to nobody that wanted nothing this time of night?

CORKY. Hard to say. No…actually, it was Sally.

TAD. My sister? I talked to her last night.

CORKY. Yeah, she was just confirming we're still coming to the wedding.

TAD. Of course, we're coming. I promised to give her away to the groom. And when I make a promise, I keep it.

CORKY. Right. And I promised to take pictures.

TAD. So, it's San Diego. By noon Sunday. Easy trip. No problem. *(beat)* It's still noon isn't it? I mean, I hate to be late for anything. And, Sally kept changing the time. First it was sunrise, and then twilight because she thought that was more romantic, then sunrise again, then she finally settled on noon Sunday. She didn't change the time again, did she?

CORKY. If that's what you remember, then that's what it is. So, I'm off to bed. Night.

*(**CORKY** exits. Pause. **TAD** stands for a moment staring sleepily.)*

TAD. *(looks at watch)* Awgh! Darn! Now I'll never get back to sleep!

(blackout)

*(After a moment the lights come up slowly. It's the next morning, a Saturday in June, about 7 a.m. There is an early morning quiet, except for a few seagulls, fog horns and dogs barking. The sun is slowly coming up over the bay, which lights the stage where there is a "car." The car is generic or modeled after any convertible style currently popular with young people. The top is down. "Wild Goose" is painted on its side. See Production Notes on "the Car." After a moment, **TAD** enters from the house. He is a serious, practical, and pessimistic "desert rat."*

He carries a small suitcase, and moves purposefully, but sleepily toward the car. Behind him, moving spryly and breezily and, swinging a small duffle bag, is **CORKY**, *a mischievous, slightly zany "beach-bum" and talented photographer. He stops, looks at the sky and yawns.)*

TAD. Come on, Corky! Hurry up! We're already behind schedule.

*(***TAD*** leans over one side of the car and carefully puts his suitcase in the back seat. From the other side of the car,* **CORKY** *casually and carelessly lobs his duffle bag into the back seat, which hits the bent over* **TAD** *on the head.)*

OW! Hey, watch it!

CORKY. Sorry, Tad. I was just trying to "hurry up."

*(***CORKY*** *smiles mischievously)*

TAD. I feel bad enough already. I didn't get back to sleep till after three.

(They begin to get into the car)

CORKY. *(brightly)* Want me to drive?

TAD. NO, NO! I'll drive. I may be tired but I'm not crazy. You navigate.

CORKY. Okay-dokay. Off to the wedding.

(He gets out map. During the next few lines **TAD** *tries to start the engine. The engine turns over briefly but doesn't start.* **TAD** *tries to start car several more times during the following. See Production Notes on casting a sound person.)*

TAD. By the way, when you talked to Sally last night, did she tell you who she was marrying?

CORKY. No. Said it was a surprise.

TAD. Sally likes secrets. She's had an off-and-on romantic engagement to Sam Simpson for six or seven months. So, I assume it's Sam. Sells insurance.

CORKY. That doesn't sound like Sally.

TAD. Never know. She does some crazy things sometimes.

Erratic and erotic – that's Sally. But, after 10 years in Hollywood and only getting bit parts in B movies, she's finally going to get married and settle down. And Mom is really glad.

CORKY. I can never really picture Sally settling down to anything. She's too spunky and full of life.

TAD. I know…too spunky for me. But she's my older sister, and since my dad isn't around much, I promised to give her away at her wedding. So, if I'm late, Mom will never forgive me.

(frustrated at car not starting)

Darn! – Disaster already! I'm not sure the "Wild Goose" will make it.

CORKY. Don't be negative, Tad. Have a little faith. Personally, I hope to have a fantastic trip…filled with romance, adventure and fun!

TAD. Romance…?

CORKY. Why not? It's a California odyssey. You never know what fate has in store for us, or when romance might come into our lives, on the way to a wedding.

TAD. Not on this trip.

CORKY. Could be. On a trip like this, anything could happen.

(The engine starts.)

There see! The engine started.

TAD. *(doubtfully)* I just want to get there in time. You always want to be late places. You think it's more exciting to dash in the last minute.

CORKY. Well, yeah, you'll have to admit it's more dramatic.

TAD. Not for me it isn't.

CORKY. Well, whatever happens, San Diego, heeeere we come!

TAD. *(He frowns, moans, and shakes his head doubtfully.)* Oh, I hope so.

*(**TAD** guns the motor and takes off with a lurch just as the lights plunge to half. This cross fades with "TIME/ TRAVEL – SOUND/MUSIC" to indicate the passage of time to a new place. This may be recorded or live, possibly with harmonica or guitar. After a moment, the lights come up again and the music fades. It is about two hours later. They are now on Highway 17, the highway to Santa Cruz. **TAD** is driving tensely. **CORKY** is in the front seat with a camera around his neck, reading a map. After a long moment **TAD** speaks.)*

TAD. Okay, Corky! Let's review the schedule.

CORKY. We just left San Francisco two hours ago. We've already reviewed it four times.

TAD. I know, but you changed it. You added this big detour on Highway 17!

CORKY. There's no big detour! We're only going to Santa Cruz so we can visit the Pacific Ocean and see the famous Boardwalk.

TAD. I hate detours.

CORKY. *(slowly reading road sign)* There see…"Fifteen miles to Santa Cruz."

TAD. If we live that long! Zig-zagging on this mountain road is suicide!

CORKY. *(casually reading another sign)* "Speed Limit 45."

TAD. Between this winding road and the fog, I'm lucky to be doing 20!

CORKY. You're actually doing about 12! And the way cars keep passing us I thought you had stopped.

TAD. I might as well.

(moaningly) Ooooh! – We'll never get to Sally's wedding by Sunday.

CORKY. At this rate of speed we won't get there till next month. Why don't you live dangerously, and speed up to 15?

(increased motor speed)

TAD. Going this way is a huge mistake. No more detours.

CORKY. Just enjoy the trip, and try not to think of it as a "package tour." Any *nor*mal person would *like* a trip filled with surprises.

TAD. Not me. All this change of schedule and running behind makes me nervous, and gives me a headache.

CORKY. Relax, Tad, and think of all the women you'll meet at Sally's wedding.

TAD. No. I'm not interested. They're all too fickle.

CORKY. You were interested in Beverly Borden of Borrego Springs?

TAD. Oh, yeah, good old Babe! Don't remind me. That's history.

CORKY. You and Babe were one hot couple.

TAD. For awhile. Yeah, she was something else. But, we had a bad ending. I'll never see her again. In fact, I'm giving up on all women for a year.

CORKY. Ha! I don't believe it. You can't resist their charms.

TAD. Sure I can. If I put my mind to it.

CORKY. Oh? Wanna bet?

TAD. You mean like a real bet?

CORKY. Yeah. No women for one full year.

TAD. Ummm…How about six months?

CORKY. Okay. Six months. It's a bet!

TAD. What do you wanna bet?

CORKY. How about our car?

TAD. "The Wild Goose…?"

CORKY. We own it 50-50. The winner gets 100%.

TAD. I don't know about giving up half of my car.

CORKY. Well, of course, if you're planning to lose. I mean, if you don't have the will power to resist some sexy woman…

TAD. Okay, okay! It's a bet!

CORKY. Shake?

TAD. Shake!

(As they shake the car swerves and at the same time some person suddenly emerges from the wings.)

CORKY. HEY, WATCH OUT!

(There's a screeching of tires and they barely miss "The Person" that is hitchhiking.)

TAD. What happened?

CORKY. You almost hit that guy.

TAD. What guy?

CORKY. Hitchhiking! Didn't you see him? STOP THE CAR!

*(**TAD** puts on the brakes and the car screeches to stop as he looks around to see what happened.)*

TAD. He must have come out of nowhere.

CORKY. *(calling back to person)* HEY! WANNA RIDE?

TAD. Aw, Corky! No hitchhikers!

CORKY. Aren't you curious about meeting new people?

TAD. NO!

*("The person" approaches the car. Her name is **JINX O'BRIEN**. She is in her mid-twenties, about the same age as **TAD** and **CORKY**. She has auburn hair in a pageboy style and fair skin. She is innocently curious, teasingly charming, and intensely personal with a hearty earthiness and tomboy quality. She wears slightly crazy or outlandish clothes which could have been bought at a thrift store. The clothes are accented by scarves and jewelry and a hat with a flower.)*

JINX. Hi, there?

CORKY. Look, Tad, he's a her!

TAD. Just my luck!

JINX. Going my way?

CORKY. Which way you going?

JINX. Santa Cruz.

CORKY. So are we. Hop in.

TAD. Not in front. It's too crowded. And, it's dangerous with this steering wheel.

JINX. Okay, I'll sit in back.

> (**JINX** *gets in back and* **TAD** *accelerates the car again.*)

This is fantastic of you guys to pick me up. I'm Jinx O'Brien.

CORKY. Corky Saylors.

TAD. Tad Miller.

JINX. You two related?

CORKY. Yes.

TAD. And no.

CORKY. We're sort of cousins by cross marriages…or something.

TAD. Corky's dad's in shipping in Long Beach. And he's a beach bum.

CORKY. And Tad's dad's in agriculture in the central valley. He's a desert rat.

JINX. Oh, good, just my luck…picked up by a bum and a rat.

> (**CORKY** *chuckles and* **TAD** *looks dour.*)

TAD. My sister Sally is getting married in San Diego on Sunday.

CORKY. Sam Simpson. Sells insurance. I'm taking the wedding pictures.

> (*raising camera*)

Smile.

> (**JINX** *gets posy and winks.* **CORKY** *clicks and* **TAD** *notices.*)

What are you doing in Santa Cruz?

TAD. Nothing. We're just passing through. We aren't staying in Santa Cruz.

JINX. Me, either. I'm looking for my dad. Ever hear of Stormy O'Brien?

> (**CORKY** *shakes his head, and mutters, "No."*)

TAD. Yeah! "King of the California Rodeos!"

JINX. That's my dad.

TAD. Stormy's the greatest. The rodeo's big in the valley. Sally's always hanging around those guys.

JINX. I haven't seen him in a long time. But an old rodeo friend of my dad's, a guy name Johnny Youngblood, is a documentary film maker, and he asked me to write a script about my dad. So, I'm looking for him.

TAD. Any clues?

JINX. No. He's always on the move. Lots of different jobs. Maybe he worked for your dads on the coast or in the desert.

CORKY. No, they only hire slave labor. We worked for them last summer.

JINX. Johnny suggested I start by talking to the carnies on the Boardwalk in Santa Cruz. He got a cowboy band, called the Western Saints, to give me a lift. But when we stopped for coffee at the Summit, I went to the ladies' room. When I came out they were gone. Abandoned me. Story of my life.

CORKY. Right. Don't go to the ladies' room.

JINX. They were all super guys, but they had other plans. Look, they gave me this jewelry.

CORKY. Um! Looks fantastic!

JINX. Thanks. I love it, 'cause it makes me feel special.

CORKY. Yeah, very special.

TAD. Very exciting.

CORKY. Tut, tut, Tad. Mustn't get too excited.

TAD. Where's your Mom?

JINX. Santa Monica. She's an actress. Does bit parts in movies. Ever see "The Monster Invades Hope Springs?"

CORKY. Saw it on the late show. She killed the monster with hair spray.

JINX. That's it. Anyway, dad didn't like Hollywood, and mom didn't like horse manure. So they split up. She became a drama teacher, dad followed the rodeo circuit, and I'm on my own.

(**TAD** *stops the car with motor decelerating and stopping.*)

TAD. Santa Cruz!

(*distant carnival sounds of an Amusement Center*)

JINX. Good. And there's the Boardwalk. I'll bet some of the carnies know him.

(**JINX** *gets out of car.*)

TAD. We can't wait while you talk to them.

JINX. Just a few questions. Please, Tad.

CORKY. Right, Tad. Man does not live by schedules alone.

JINX. I won't be long. I promise. Okay…?

TAD. Well, maybe…if you don't stay too long.

JINX. Thanks. What a nice guy.

(**JINX** *runs off toward amusement center.*)

TAD. She'll stay too long. I know she will.

CORKY. (*looking at roller coaster*) Wow! That roller coaster looks like fun!

TAD. We don't have time for fun! We're running late.

(*looking after* **JINX** *nervously*)

Uh, listen, Corky…what if we ditch her.

CORKY. Not on your life. Jinx seems like somebody special.

TAD. Hey! I think you're falling in love already! What a romantic!

(**CORKY** *smiles and shrugs. Cross fade lights to Board-walk Concession area. A* **CARNIVAL BARKER** *is working on something in front of his concession booth.* **JINX** *approaches him.*)

JINX. Hey, Mister, could you…

BARKER. Sorry, young lady, we're not open yet.

JINX. I know. I'm looking for somebody. You know Stormy O'Brien?

BARKER. Stormy O'Brien? Oh, yeah, we all know Stormy. Why you lookin' for him?

JINX. Well, I'm his daughter, and I…

BARKER. His daughter!

(The **BARKER** *motions to* **TWO WOMEN CARNVIAL WORKERS**.*)*

Hey, Girls, listen to this. This here's Stormy's kid. She's lookin' for her old man.

(The **TWO WOMEN CARNIVAL WORKERS** *move toward* **JINX**. **WOMAN CARNIE #1** *is a large, outgoing, forthright woman. And* **WOMAN CARNIE #2** *is a small, snippy, snide and suspicious person.)*

WOMAN CARNIE #2. You ain't the only one.

WOMAN CARNIE #1. Whatcha want with Stormy?

WOMAN CARNIE #2. I hope he didn't promise you nothin', Honey.

JINX. No, no. It's just that I haven't seen him for a long time, and I sort of forget what he was like.

BARKER. Whatcha wanna know?

WOMAN CARNIE #1. We can tell you.

WOMAN CARNIE #2. We know him real good.

JINX. Well, I sort of remember him as a big, strong, handsome man.

BARKER. He was handsome all right. Not reeeeal tall.

WOMAN CARNIE #1. But strong as an ox.

BARKER. And tough as nails.

WOMAN CARNIE #2. He just seemed bigger 'cause he was the loud, out-goin' type.

WOMAN CARNIE #1. Yeah, bigger than life!

BARKER. He mostly worked on the Merry-Go-Round.

WOMAN CARNIE #1. Loved the horses. Made up stories about 'em. Gave 'em all a name.

WOMAN CARNIE #2. Reminded him of the rodeo.

BARKER. He had a wicked sense of humor. Real practical joker.

WOMAN CARNIE #1. Remember the time he changed the speed on the merry-go-round so all the horses ran like bucking broncos?

(They all begin to chuckle.)

BARKER. And the time he fixed Bing's Shooting Gallery so all the ducks fell down.

(They all laugh a bit more.)

WOMAN CARNIE #1. Great story teller, too. And he loved cowboy movies.

WOMAN CARNIE #2. Kept braggin' how he could make better cowboy movies than all them other Hollywood directors if he just had the chance.

BARKER. Had a guitar, too. Used to serenade all the good lookin' gals.

WOMAN CARNIE #1. They loved Stormy. Fell all over themselves.

WOMAN CARNIE #2. Some did, some didn't.

*(****CORKY**** enters cheerfully in the background carrying a teddy bear with* **TAD** *moping along behind looking very grumpy. They move into the scene just in time to hear the following.)*

WOMAN CARNIE #1. Yeah, that's right. But…Stormy O'Brien was a born con man.

CORKY. *(quietly appalled)* "Con man!"

BARKER. One of the best.

CORKY. (**CORKY** *nods knowingly, realizing this is a "compliment" and says softly.)* Right! One in a million.

JINX. Know where he is now?

WOMAN CARNIE #1. No idea. But, he won't be comin' 'round here again real soon.

JINX. Why not?

WOMAN CARNIE #2. Wouldn't dare. If he knows what's good for him.

BARKER. That's right.

WOMAN CARNIE #1. We all trusted him for awhile, but, then…

BARKER. He disappeared owin' lotsa folks money.

WOMAN CARNIE #2. He could be anyplace by now.

WOMAN CARNIE #1. Yeah, but come to think of it, Jinx…he was always talkin' about seein' you again.

BARKER. That's right. He carried around some kind of mysterious treasure box he said he was savin' for you.

JINX. Me…?! A treasure box?

WOMAN CARNIE #1. Yeah. And he sometimes talked about his relatives near King City.

JINX. Oh, that's Aunt Lita and Uncle Herman. I need to see them.

WOMAN CARNIE #2. Well, I don't care if he is your dad…if I was you, honey, I wouldn't have nothin' to do with Stormy. He's big trouble.

TAD. *(tapping his watch)* Uh, speaking of trouble, we have to go now.

JINX. Thanks for all the information.

*(As the **CARNIVAL WORKERS** move off, they ad-lib.)*

BARKER: Good luck to you, honey.

WOMAN CARNIE #1: Hope you find him…if that's what you want.

WOMAN CARNIE #2: Don't forget to take care of yourself.

TAD. Ready?

CORKY. Soon as I take one picture.

TAD. Come on, Corky, this has taken too much time already.

*(**CORKY** hands the Teddy Bear to **JINX** and begins to play with his camera. **TAD** moans.)*

Ooooh, what next?

JINX. *(handing the bear to **TAD**)* I think Taddy should hold Teddy.

*(**TAD** groans, but is slightly pleased at the attention. They put their heads together. **CORKY** holds the camera out in front of them.)*

CORKY. 1…2…

*(**CORKY** smiles broadly, **TAD** frowns and **JINX** winks. They freeze. **CORKY** clicks camera. The lights fade on them.)*

*(TIME PASSING TRAVEL MUSIC. After a few moments, the lights again come up and they are back in the car. It is several hours later, about 11 a.m. **TAD** is driving. The teddy bear is in the front seat with **TAD**. **CORKY** is in the backseat with **JINX**.)*

*(At the moment **CORKY** is looking at the countryside through his camera lens. **JINX** is writing notes on a pad for her movie. **CORKY** stands up in the car and aims his camera at some farm workers.)*

JINX. What're you doing?

CORKY. Photographing farm workers.

TAD. Corky made a documentary about California farm workers. Won a prize.

JINX. Congratulations. I'd like to see it sometime.

> *(Just then, **TAD** turns a corner and **CORKY** weaves unsurely.)*

JINX. OOoooH! – Watch out…!

> *(**CORKY** falls into seat against **JINX**. They are very close.)*

CORKY. Hi, there.

JINX. Hi, yourself.

CORKY. Did I tell you I think you're special?

JINX. Several times. But it's always nice to hear it again.

TAD. *(announcing like a tour guide)* Kiiiing Ciiiity.

> *(**JINX** mutters an, "Oh!")*

CORKY. Looks like the king's out of town.

JINX. Keep going. Aunt Lita's Cafe's on the outskirts.

CORKY. Who's Aunt Lita?

JINX. She's not really my aunt. She's more like my dad's girlfriend. She and her daughter Zulie run the Swan Cafe. It's next door to Uncle Herman's Post Office.

CORKY. What if they don't know anything about your dad?

JINX. I'll find him. I have relatives all over California.

TAD. We're not going *all over* California. We're going to San Diego.

JINX. I should stop by Mom's place in Santa Monica. Only she's mad at me.

CORKY. Why?

JINX. Because, well…she wanted me to stay home. But, I figured if mom and dad were never home, why should I have to stay. So, I kept running off…having adventures of my own. Some of my best friends are strangers.

CORKY. I can relate to that. But, didn't you tell them you were leaving?

JINX. How can you say goodbye to someone who's never there? Mom thinks I'm really wild.

CORKY. Are you?

JINX. I don't think so. I've had lots of fun, but I've never felt guilty about anything. Does that shock you?

CORKY. Not me. I like to get involved with unusual people like you, Jinx O'Brien.

JINX. I'm just curious about life.

CORKY. I'm curious too…about you.

JINX. If there's anything I can do to repay you for helping me find my dad, just let me know.

CORKY. What'd you have in mind?

JINX. (**JINX** *smiles teasingly.*) Now, now, don't be naughty.

> (*They look in each other's eyes, get close and "snugly." Seeing this in the rear view mirror,* **TAD** *swerves the car off the highway with the sound of squealing tires, then pulls up to the Post Office and Cafe, jams on the brakes with the sound of screeching tires and stops, jerking them forward.*)

TAD. Swan Café!

JINX. Look, we're here!. Come on, you guys, follow me.

> (**JINX** *crosses toward Swan Café at stage left.* **CORKY** *starts to follow and* **TAD** *grabs him.*)

TAD. Listen, Corky, if you think I'm going to play chauffeur all the way to San Diego while you and Jinxie play "mousy" in the back seat, you're crazy!

CORKY. Now, now, Tad, remember, you're not having anything to do with women. But that doesn't mean I can't.

(**CORKY** *smiles and moves into stage area of the Swan Cafe as* **TAD** *fumes, "AGH!" and follows. The lights come up to reveal the Swan Café. This is a small, rural roadside restaurant with a counter, a couple of stools a table with chairs, signs on the wall, and an archway into the post office. No one is in sight.* **JINX** *enters followed by* **CORKY** *and* **TAD**.)

JINX. *(calling out)* Isn't anybody in charge of this joint?

(*Just then,* **UNCLE HERMAN** *enters wearing a green eyeshade with some mail in his hand. He's a hearty, friendly and burly sort of man in his late 40s to early 50s.*)

HERMAN. Sorry. I was sorting out some... – Well, I'll be jiggered! If it isn't Jinx! Ho, ho!

(*He gives her a big hug.* **AUNT LITA** *enters from the kitchen area. She's in her mid-40s. She has naturally lovely features that have faded a bit from a difficult life.*)

LITA. Listen, Herman, don't you deliver that mail till I've read it. You hear?

HERMAN. Lita, you gotta quit readin' other folks' mail.

LITA. I gotta have *some* fun in this God-forsaken place.

JINX. Hi, Aunt Lita.

LITA. *(seeing* **JINX** *and others)* I'll be a horse's rear end, if it ain't my baby Jinx!

(*hugging* **JINX**)

And who're these good lookin' fellows?

JINX. These are my friends, Tad Miller...

TAD. Pleased to meet you, Aunt Lita.

LITA. Just call me Lita, honey.

JINX. ...And Corky Saylors.

CORKY. Hi, Lita honey.

(**ZULIE,** **LITA**'s *daughter, who has freckles, red hair and pigtails, enters from kitchen.*)

ZULIE. Hey, Mom, I just sneezed in the soup of the day.

LITA. This here's Zulie. She's got a cold.

> (**ZULIE** *smiles and waves. Then she sneezes and blows her nose.*)

LITA. How 'bout some food for you fellahs?

CORKY. Food, good! But I'm allergic to soup of the day.

ZULIE. And there's no more tuna fish. But you don't have to feed the cat.

LITA. How 'bout some sandwiches?

CORKY. Fine! Peanut butter – jelly. Old dog biscuits. Anything!

TAD. But we're kind of in a hurry 'cause we're running behind schedule.

LITA. How 'bout I pack 'em for the road?

CORKY, TAD & JINX *(ad-libbing)* YEAH! Good idea! That'd be nice.

TAD. And we need some gas.

HERMAN. Help yourself. Any friend of Jinx' gets one tank at half price.

TAD. Thanks. That's really nice of you.

> (**TAD** *and* **CORKY** *exit.*)

LITA. Honey, what brings you 'round to these parts?

JINX. I'm looking for my dad, to find out some things about his life.

ZULIE. If you want to know all about your dad, Mom can tell you lotsa good stories.

LITA. Jinx honey, your dad…John Patrick "Stormy" O'Brien…is a red-headed, freckled faced, pug-nosed Irishman, who's a hard-working, hard-drinking, hot-tempered cowboy…

HERMAN. A guy with a great sense of humor who loves practical jokes.

LITA. People always love Stormy 'cause he can be one of the most charmin', devilish kind of guys you ever want to meet.

ZULIE. Mom's got a thing for him.

LITA. When he gets all slickered up, he can be one hunk of a good-lookin' man.

HERMAN. Stormy's not only a woman's man, but he's also a rodeo man. He can do it all. He's the king.

ZULIE. He's best at throwing the bull.

LITA. Zulie never liked the way he was always struttin' 'round like a cock-of-the-walk.

ZULIE. The three of 'em used to get all dressed up in matching western outfits. Yuck!

LITA. Lord knows Stormy's not perfect. He spent money like it was going out of style.

HERMAN. But folks always want to give Stormy another chance. I think he secretly wanted to be in the movies.

JINX. Dad…?

HERMAN. Even had some offers.

LITA. But your mom was in the movies, and he didn't want to compete with her 'cause she was a real actress.

JINX. So, where is he now?

HERMAN. Don't know. But early this year Stormy got hurt pretty bad.

LITA. I told him he oughta quit rodeoin' and do somethin' else, 'cause that was a young man's game. That made him mad. Said he could still rodeo with the best of 'em – young or not! We had a terrible bad fight about that.

ZULIE. A whopper!

HERMAN. Then, he left, and we ain't seen hide nor hair of him since.

LITA. But he'd like to see you again, Jinx. I know…'cause he talked about you all the time.

JINX. He did?

HERMAN. Fact is, he left a Treasure Box for you. Got it right here.

(**HERMAN** *moves off just as* **TAD** *and* **CORKY** *come back in the front door.*)

TAD. Okay, I'm full of gas.

CORKY. And, so is the car.

> (**HERMAN** *returns with the Treasure Box.* **JINX** *immediately and eagerly focuses in on the box and the carvings on the lid.*)

JINX. Wow! Look at all the strange little creatures on the lid. OOOoooh, they're dancing.

HERMAN. They represent the seven deadly sins.

CORKY. Hey, neat!

JINX. It's beautiful!

TAD. I think it's weird.

ZULIE. Yeah, hideous.

CORKY. *(smiling deliciously)* A touch of evil!

JINX. Yes! It smells all sweet like cloves or mint…or something exotic. And here's a little golden key that opens the box. I wonder what's inside.

HERMAN. Don't open it. It's secret.

LITA. Stormy told us it represented all the things that are past memories in his life.

JINX. Oh, I'm so curious I can't wait to open it.

HERMAN. Don't you dare. Never ever. Or there's serious consequences.

JINX. "Never ever…?"

LITA. Not unless something really bad happens to Stormy.

JINX. You mean, like if he died?

HERMAN. Those were our instructions. If you open the box before that happens, you will release all the sins of the world.

JINX. Ooooh, doesn't that sound exciting?

LITA. That's a warning. So beware!

JINX. I don't know if I can control myself. Aren't you guys curious?

CORKY. I am. Wow!

TAD. Not me. If her dad said, "Don't open it," I have no temptation.

(looking at watch)

TAD. Hey, we need to leave.

JINX. I don't want to leave without it.

HERMAN. I can't give you this Treasure Box unless you promise not to open it.

TAD. *(raising his hand like taking an oath)* Okay, I'll promise to guard it.

HERMAN. And keep Jinx from opening it?

TAD. Sure, sure. I promise.

CORKY. And when Tad makes a promise he keeps it.

TAD. Right. Whatever happens.

CORKY. Right.

HERMAN. Well, then, I'll just give the Treasure Box to this responsible young man for safe-keeping. You're now in charge.

*(**CORKY** smiles knowingly as **HERMAN** takes Treasure Box out of **JINX**'s hands and gives it to **TAD**.)*

JINX. Good, Tad. You can help me resist my temptations.

TAD. Oh, yeah, well…right. No problem. But, right now we need to go.

LITA. And here's some snacks for you kids.

*(**LITA** hands large bags of food to **CORKY**.)*

CORKY. I'll handle those.

*(**CORKY** eagerly takes the food. They all move out of the Cafe with ad-libs of appreciation as lights come up on the car area.)*

JINX: Thanks for everything.

TAD: Yeah! The gas.

CORKY: And the food!

*(They get in the car, as **LITA**, **HERMAN** and **ZULIE** wave goodbye and overlap.)*

HERMAN: Good luck. Have a good trip!

LITA: Hope you find Stormy.

ZULIE: Come back again.

(As **TAD** *starts the engine, the lights fade on the café. Then, as they accelerate, the lights fade to half and TIME TRAVEL MUSIC increases to indicate passage of time to a new place. After a few moments, the lights come up fully again on* **CORKY**, **TAD** *and* **JINX**. *It's about an hour later.* **TAD** *is tensely hunched over the wheel and frowning.* **CORKY** *and* **JINX** *are in the back seat together.* **CORKY** *is looking at a map.)*

CORKY. Fifteen miles to San Luis Obispo.

TAD. Oh, no! We're way behind schedule. We should be in Santa Barbara by now. It's all because I have to worry about that Treasure Box.

JINX. Oh, Tad, I know. And I'm sorry, because you're a very mature and sensible person, and I really admire that.

CORKY. Me, too. We all do, Tad.

JINX. But, oh my…When I look at this beautiful Treasure Box, I just wonder what could possibly be…I mean… I'm just bursting with curiosity to know what's inside.

TAD. Okay, okay, I know what you're doing. You can't fool me. You're conniving to open that box.

CORKY. I think you should satisfy your curiosity.

TAD. Remember…curiosity killed the cat.

CORKY. But satisfaction brought it back.

JINX. That's right.

TAD. Don't encourage her, Corky.

CORKY. Go ahead, Jinx…follow your instincts. Open it.

TAD. Oh, no, you don't!

CORKY. Who's to stop her?

TAD. *I* am! I'm responsible for it.

JINX. I don't see how I can possibly resist my temptations much longer.

CORKY. Then, go ahead. Open it! Or, I'll open it!

TAD. Oh, no you don't! Over my dead body!

CORKY. Now *I'm really* tempted.

TAD. Agh, my neck. I'm getting a splitting headache.

JINX. It sounds to me like a simple case of stress and tension.

CORKY. With Tad nothing is simple.

TAD. It's all because I have to do all the driving, and keep up the schedules. And now I have to worry about you and that Treasure Box!

CORKY. Want me to drive?

TAD. NO! My head hurts, but I'm not crazy!

CORKY. Hmmm. Running behind schedule upsets Tad's whole system. When Tad gets all tense and nervous like this he gets constipated.

TAD. I'm *not* constipated! OOOoooh, my head!

CORKY. And when he gets seriously uptight he can go into convulsions, roll on the ground, and foam at the mouth.

JINX. Is that really true?

TAD. NO, NO, NO!

CORKY. Absolutely. He becomes "Mad Tad Miller."

TAD. Okay, THAT DOES IT!

> (**TAD** *jams on the brakes with the sound of tires screeching to a stop.* **TAD** *pulls over to stop and turns off motor.*)

CORKY. *(after a tense pause, hesitantly)* Uh…I didn't think we were going to stop in San Luis Obispo. And, this is "Emergency Parking Only."

TAD. *(seething and angry)* Yeah, well this is an emergency!

CORKY. *(innocently)* I don't know why you're so upset.

TAD. Because you keep trying to get my goat.

CORKY. *(innocently)* Why Tad, I didn't even know you *had* a goat.

TAD. THERE! – SEE! You did it again!

CORKY. Tad, you've got a serious case of "seriousness."

JINX. You just need to relax and have more fun!

CORKY. Right, Tad. More fun.

TAD. Life is not all fun and giggles!

CORKY. Now that's very profound! Say it again, and I'll take your picture.

(CORKY raises his camera and TAD narrows his eyes and snarls)

TAD. GRRRRRR!! YOU'RE NEVER GOING TO GROW UP!

JINX. Now, now, Tad! You're losing control.

TAD. I can't help it. He DRIVES ME CRAZY!

CORKY. Now, now, I wouldn't admit that publicly.

TAD. OUT! Get OUT of the car!

(CORKY gets out hesitantly. TAD spars with his fists.)

Okay, okay! Now put 'em up or shut up!

CORKY. *(toughly)* Okay, buddy, okay! There's no decision there! *(beat)* I'll shut up.

(CORKY "locks his lips" and throws away the "key.")

My lips are sealed.

(He picks up his camera, and begins to move away.)

See you guys later.

TAD. Hey! Where're you going?

CORKY. To take pictures of the Mission.

TAD. THE MISSION! There's no time.

CORKY. *(to JINX)* Want to come?

JINX. No, thanks. I have a mission right here.

(She motions toward TAD and winks. CORKY waves and heads off.)

CORKY. Later.

TAD. HEY! WE DON'T HAVE TIME TO TAKE PICTURES OF THE MISSION! We're already behind schedule! – COR-KY?!

(seeing CORKY is gone)

TAD. *(cont.)* Ugh! Sometimes he really upsets me!

JINX. *(soothingly)* Oh, I know. He can be so irritating at times.

TAD. Ugh! We'll *never* get to San Diego in time for the wedding. Now I've got a terrible headache.

JINX. Poor Tad. You have all those responsibilities. All the driving, and worrying about my Treasure Box…

TAD. Yeah, that's true. I can't do it all.

JINX. No. It's just too much for one person. Come on. Get back in the car.

(**TAD** *gets back as she continues to talk.*)

Sit here beside me…just relax…and let me rub those shoulders. Get rid of all that nasty tension.

(*She begins to rub his shoulders.*)

TAD. Oooh, but when I think how Corky keeps putting us behind schedule…!

JINX. Oh, I know. He needs to be much more appreciative of all you're doing on his trip.

TAD. Ugh! But sometimes he gets under my skin…and really irritates me! And sometimes…when I think how he…uh…Hey…whooo, that feels good.

JINX. (*soothingly*) You just need to relax and let go.

TAD. Okay, I'm relaxing…

JINX. Isn't this a lot better?

(*massaging his temples*)

TAD. Ooooooooh, yes, that feels sooooo good! Ummm… and I'm letting go….and I'm liking it. (*sigh*)

JINX. You know, Tad, I think you and I are going to get along very well. Very well indeed.

TAD. Ummmm, so do I. Just keep rubbing.

(*He smiles a wilting, relaxed smile as the lights slowly fade. After a moment, out of the darkness, we hear a bell from the bell tower in the mission: BONG! BONG! CLANG! After another brief moment, the lights come up and* **TAD** *and* **JINX** *are still sitting in the car. It is sometime later, but* **JINX** *is still massaging* **TAD**'s *shoulders, neck and temples.* **TAD** *is sort of drifting…half asleep. She stops massaging and shakes her fingers.*)

TAD. Ummmm…don't stop.

JINX. I had to. My fingers went numb.

(*Suddenly,* **TAD** *is jarred back to reality. He sits up, checks his watch and looks around.*)

TAD. Oh, darn! Where could Corky be? We've got to get this show on the road. OOOh! – I just got another pain in my head.

JINX. Now, Tad, you mustn't keep upsetting yourself. That's what's causing your tension headaches. People driving with headaches can cause accidents. So, when Corky comes back, there's no reason why he can't drive.

TAD. No, no! Bad idea. He's erratic and dangerous. OH, MY HEAD!

JINX. But if he drives, you can relax back here with me. What do you think?

(**CORKY** *approaches casually, smiling and carrying a brown bag with fruit in it.*)

CORKY. Hi, ho! I have returned!

TAD. WHERE!…Where have you been!?

CORKY. Taking pictures of the Mission.

TAD. That was 45 minutes ago!

CORKY. I took an unguided tour, and got lost in the bell tower. But I had fun ringing the bell until the Nuns dragged me off the rope.

TAD. They what? I don't believe that! Listen, Corky, you wasted a lot of time doing that. And we're running way behind schedule.

CORKY. Time goes fast when you're having fun. Apparently you weren't.

TAD. I WAS, TOO!

CORKY. Here, I brought you some freshly picked fruit from the orchards of California.

JINX. (*taking bag*) "Fresh fruit…?"

TAD. Jinx and I decided it was your turn to drive.

CORKY. Oh, okay, sure. No problem.

(*He gets in car.*)

CORKY. Let's see now…Is this the doo-hickey they call the steering wheel?

TAD. Quit acting dumb!

JINX. Brrrr, I'm freezing. Can we put the top up?

TAD. No, it's, uh…broken.

CORKY. It used to work fine. But then, one day it acted dumb, and Tad lost his temper and…Powee! – Broken!

TAD. Ignore him.

> (**TAD** *opens up a blanket and spreads it over their legs.*)

Here, try this.

JINX. Ummmm, nice and cozy.

CORKY. Hold on, Lovebirds. Here we go.

> (**CORKY** *starts the engine and accelerates jerkily and they all jerk back and forth rhythmically.*)

JINX. Have you been driving long?

CORKY. I'm a little out of practice.

TAD. He's just doing that on purpose.

CORKY. Hang on. I'll get the hang of it yet.

> (*He slowly accelerates and the lights slowly fade to half. TIME TRAVEL SOUND MUSIC. After a moment, The lights come up to full. It is a couple of hours later.* **TAD** *and* **JINX** *are under the blanket in the back seat.* **CORKY** *is still driving. He looks in the rearview mirror, smiles, and after a moment of thought starts talking like a movie reviewer.*)

Good evening, Mr. and Mrs. Movie-Goer. This is Corky Lens, your favorite Hollywood Reporter reviewing the new X-rated movie: *Love Under A Blanket* with some of the hottest scenes ever filmed. No love-starved fan should miss this titillating, fun-filled romantic scene, now showing in our local back seat. Thank you and good night from Hollywood.

JINX. (*peeking out from under blanket*) Nothing is "showing." We're just trying to stay warm.

CORKY. Far be it from me to break up one hot romance.

(**TAD** *lowers the blanket. He has a giant lipstick imprint on his cheek, which* **CORKY** *sees in the rearview mirror.*)

TAD. Pay attention to your driving.

CORKY. Ah! I see you're wearing the mark of "The Big Kissers."

(**TAD** *rubs vigorously to remove the lipstick that is on his cheek.*)

TAD. No big deal.

JINX. "No big deal?!"

CORKY. You mean, you're going to deny you've fallen in love again?

TAD. Well, no, not exactly.

JINX. "Again?" What's that mean?

TAD. Nothing. Just a little wager we had. Ignore it.

CORKY. "Nothing…?! You mean, you have no real feelings for Jinx?

TAD. *(caught uneasily between* **CORKY** *and* **JINX***)* Oh, yeah, sure, of course I do.

CORKY. Ah, well then, does that mean…or could you say you have romantic feelings for Jinx?

(**JINX** *looks at* **TAD** *sweetly and smiles innocently, waiting for his answer.*)

JINX. I hope so, Tad…after all I've done for your tension.

TAD. Uh, yeah well, uh…I guess you could say that.

(**JINX** *mutters, "Oh, that's nice."*)

CORKY. Yes, nice. Very good! Then, the "Wild Goose" is mine!

TAD. Hey, wait a minute!

CORKY. You're not going to deny it, are you?

(*Pause.* **JINX** *looks at him.* **TAD** *is trapped.*)

TAD. Okay, okay! The car's yours!

(**CORKY** *smiles smugly.* **TAD** *smiles at* **JINX** *and says possessively.*)

TAD. But Jinx is mine.

JINX. Whoa there, Tad, I need to warn you…nobody owns me.

(putting Treasure Box on her lap)

But, we do have a great deal in common…like my Treasure Box, for instance. Ummm…It smells all sweet and tangy. And rubbing this carved wood feels sooo good…almost like velvet.

(harp chords)

Ooooh, hear that?

CORKY. *I* did! A harp!

JINX. YES!

TAD. I didn't hear anything.

JINX. It's like magic. Oh, yes, this is exciting!

TAD. Well, don't get too excited.

JINX. *(reading letters on box)* "Whoever opens me, opens a new world." Oh, I can hardly resist.

TAD. Well, try. Rubbing and smelling are okay. But opening that box is a no-no.

JINX. Oh, Tad, please!

TAD. No! I promised your Uncle Herman I would guard the box.

JINX. What harm would it do?

CORKY. It's not on Tad's schedule.

JINX. If you really, really care for me…

TAD. *(trying to change subject)* Hey, Corky, where are we?

CORKY. No idea.

TAD. Are we lost?

CORKY. No, no, we're on, uh…Pacific Highway…or 101 or 405 or someplace. *(beat)* Hey, Lovebirds, I think we're lost.

TAD. Well, wherever we are there's a bunch of palm trees, and there's the ocean.

CORKY. Anybody recognize that beach?

JINX. Oh! We're in Santa Monica. Turn left. *(beat)* And look, there's Hope Avenue where Mom lives. And there's her trailer park...the Elysian Fields. Turn in here.

(**CORKY** *turns car and decelerates.*)

JINX. There it is...there's Mom's place.

(*Car stops.* **JINX** *gets out of car.*)

Wish me luck.

(*As she hurries offstage to* **MARGO**'s *mobile home,* **CORKY** *and* **TAD** *look after her for a moment.*)

CORKY. Having fun?

TAD. Yeah! She's something else.

CORKY. I knew you couldn't resist. So, the car is mine.

TAD. Okay, okay. But, before you get too smug, you want to make another bet?

CORKY. On what?

TAD. The Treasure Box.

CORKY. What's that mean? What's the bet?

TAD. That you can't resist opening it.

CORKY. Oh, sure. No problem.

TAD. Or...if you, in any way, tempt Jinx or help Jinx...or in any way collaborate in opening that box, you lose. And I get the car back.

CORKY. Half the car.

TAD. Okay, half the car.

CORKY. It's a bet!

(*They shake hands. Lights fade on stage with car and come up to reveal* **MARGO LOVEJOY**'s *mobile home.* **JINX** *knocks on the door. No answer. She tries to look in. Then, she cautiously enters the mobile home. It is a small area, which looks like a parlor of a fortune-teller. No one is there. There is a murmur of voices offstage.* **JINX** *sees a small dinner bell on the shelf, picks it up and rings the bell. The offstage voices cease. Then, suddenly there is a loud, haughty, trance-like almost chanting voice.*)

MARGO. *(unseen)* WELCOME TO MADAME MARGO'S

FORTUNE TELLING STUDIO! PLEASE BE SEATED!

(After a moment, a gong is sounded. Then, **MARGO LOVEJOY** *enters. She is a fairly large "dramatic looking" woman in her late 40s. She wears a Gypsy fortune-teller costume with colorful turban. Her eyes are closed and arms extended.)*

MARGO. *(overly dramatic)* MARGO THE MAGNIFICENT GREETS YOU!

JINX. Hi, Mom, how you doing?

*(**MARGO** is startled and opens her eyes widely. From this point on she is very real.)*

MARGO. Heavens to Betsy, it's my very own Jinx! Where've you been all this time?

JINX. You name it. I've been there.

MARGO. *(calling off)* Hey, Rosie, come in here and meet my daughter.

(turning back to **JINX***)*

Listen, if you recognize Rosie as the actress who does the kitty litter commercials, don't mention it. How long you going to be here?

JINX. I'm just passing through.

MARGO. You've got to stay for at least a couple of days.

JINX. Mom, I can't.

MARGO. Always running away! Still wild as ever!

*(**ROSIE** enters. She is a spry, witty little woman in her late 50s.)*

ROSIE. Margo, we've got to get to work, or we won't have a job.

MARGO. Rosie, this is my daughter Jinx.

ROSIE. OH!…JINX! The bright, independent daughter you're always bragging about.

MARGO. No, this is the wild one that keeps running away.

ROSIE. Glad to meet you. Listen, Margo, we've gotta get to the theatre.

JINX. Theatre! Are you two in a play?

ROSIE. No, we just sell popcorn at the Roxie. They show famous old movies.

MARGO. Well, the whole world's a stage.

ROSIE. Margo, we gotta go. It's your turn to heat up the popcorn while I sign the photographs of famous old stars.

(**MARGO** *begins to take off her turban and robe to get ready to go to work.*)

JINX. Mom, I'm looking for Dad.

MARGO. WHY…?!

JINX. I'm writing a story about his life.

ROSIE. Now there's a wild story.

MARGO. *(self-dramatizing)* What about *my* life? The story of Margo Lovejoy – a young girl filled with talent and hope – who, on the threshold of a brilliant Hollywood career, married a charming and worthless cowboy.

JINX. Mom, it's not fiction.

MARGO. "Fiction…?!"

JINX. It's Dad's true story.

ROSIE. That's too hot to handle.

JINX. It's a movie script.

MARGO. OH! – Men always get the best roles.

ROSIE. But your mom was a magnificent actress.

MARGO. *(falsely modest)* Now, Rosie, not really "magnificent."

ROSIE. Come on, Margo, nobody likes cold popcorn.

JINX. So, what was Dad really like?

MARGO. To be perfectly honest, and more than fair, Stormy O'Brien was a charming, *un*dependable, *un*predictable, and *un*faithful ne'er-do-well. When Stormy O'Brien initialed his belt buckle "S.O.B."…that was the real man!

ROSIE. That's the truth! As both husband and father, he was a mighty good rodeo man.

MARGO. Jinx, the night you were born, he won a rodeo in Fresno, then went out to some bar with his old buddy, Spit Partch, the prospector, and his "good friend" Lita. He didn't see you till you were three years old.

JINX. Oh, Mom, you're exaggerating!

MARGO. Not much. He wanted a boy so badly is why he called you "Jinx."

JINX. Okay, Mom, okay. But where is he now?

MARGO. Who knows?

ROSIE. He called last week. Tell her.

MARGO. No. I'm not going to tell her, because she's not going to stay.

ROSIE. Now, that's what I call tacky.

JINX. Mom, if you don't tell me where Dad is, I may never come back again.

MARGO. All right, Jinx, all right. The last I heard from Stormy was when he called six days ago to wish me a happy anniversary – which was three weeks late. He was in a small town south of the Salton Sea…doing some rodeo.

JINX. El Centro? Brawley?

MARGO. No, no, I think it was…that's it…Brawley. Said he was going to be there till tomorrow.

JINX. Where's he going after that?

MARGO. Heaven only knows. Listen, Jinx, I miss you, honey. So, come see me again, sometime soon, when you can stay longer.

JINX. Thanks, Mom.

MARGO. Close the door when you leave. Oh, and Jinx…if you find your father, tell the S.O.B. – he STILL OWES ME BACK ALIMONY!

(**ROSIE** *and* **MARGO** *exit.* **JINX** *chuckles. Lights fade on* margo's *area, and come up on area with car.* **TAD** *looks at his watch.*)

TAD. Where's Jinx? She's taking longer than I thought. If we keep stopping we'll never make it.

CORKY. *(teasingly)* We could ditch her.

TAD. Not on you life! Not now! I want to take her to Sally's wedding as my date.

(Pause, while he thinks about her impact.)

Yeah. It'll just be a short, relaxed trip down the coast in the morning and we should be in San Diego by nine-thirty or ten easily. Which is none too soon for the wedding at noon. I just hope the rear tire doesn't explode.

*(**JINX** hurries in excitedly.)*

JINX. Hey, you guys, guess what? I found out where my dad is.

CORKY. Great! Where?

JINX. Near Brawley.

TAD. "BRAWLEY?!" That's east of here – in the desert.

JINX. It's just a little detour.

TAD. "Little detour?!" It's 118 miles to Brawley! And 118 degrees when we get there! And, we're not going, so forget it!

CORKY. We could go to Brawley *after* the wedding.

JINX. He won't be there *after* the wedding. This is my only chance to find my dad and write the script.

TAD. But, my sister Sally is…

JINX. I know! Your Sister Sally is getting married in San Diego on Sunday! You told me and told me…*several* times.

TAD. Yeah, well, I've got to be there because I'm giving her away.

CORKY. And Tad is very task oriented.

TAD. Right! We're not going to Brawley!

CORKY. Now don't be unreasonable, Tad.

TAD. Listen, Jinx, when you go into the hot desert territory on a summer's day, things can happen. The sun is so hot your brain gets fried and your mind plays tricks on reality. You imagine you're meeting the strangest people in the strangest places doing the strangest things. It's weird…really weird. You know what I mean?

JINX. No, not really. I'm a Bay Area girl myself.

TAD. Ah, well! Some people have hallucinations of strange things that happen to them…an almost surreal experience. And they never recover.

JINX. Ooooh, doesn't that sound exciting!

TAD. Well, it all depends. But, I don't think you'd like it. In fact, I'd strongly advise against it…if you know what's good for you.

JINX. But, I just love new experiences. And, I'm always curious.

TAD. Okay. Think of it this way…what if the car broke down in the desert? Then, you wouldn't be able to find your dad, Corky wouldn't be able to take pictures of the wedding, and I couldn't keep my promise to Sally. So, I have to be cautious about changing our plans.

CORKY. Right. So, listen, I've got an idea. If Tad is cautious and Jinx is curious then I have a plan for compromise.

TAD. What do you mean, "compromise?"

CORKY. Listen…If we sleep a couple of hours now, head into the desert about three in the morning, find Stormy in Brawley, then circle back through the mountains to San Diego, we could still get to the wedding just in the nick of time.

TAD. No, no, no. That's crazy! The back tire is about to blow out, so we sure can't make a six-hour trip through the hot desert. We can't make it.

CORKY. Sure we can. Come on, Tad. This young lady is desperate. It's another exciting adventure.

TAD. It's too exciting for me. I don't need an adventure of driving into the hot desert, and a dramatic arrival at my sister's wedding "just in the nick of time."

CORKY. *(after a thoughtful pause)* Is that your final answer?

TAD. Yes! The answer is NO! And THAT'S FINAL!

(long pause)

JINX. You know, Tad, I think you're absolutely right. Listen, you guys have been great. But, I understand. What I want to do is too much trouble.

TAD. I'm glad you understand why I can't go that way.

JINX. I do. And it's unfair of me to ask.

(Slight pause. They look at each other.)

CORKY. Wait a minute, Tad! I know what it is. I know why you don't want to go. It's Babe, isn't it?

JINX. Who's Babe?

TAD. Never mind. Nobody.

CORKY. His old girlfriend. Tad's old flame.

TAD. "Flame" hardly describes Babe.

CORKY. Tad doesn't want to see her again. Right…?

*(**JINX** is taking the Treasure Box out of the car.)*

TAD. *(trying to change subject)* Hey, what're you doing with the Treasure Box?

JINX. It's mine. If we're going separate ways then I need to take it with me.

TAD. But I promised I'd guard it, and protect it, and stop you from opening it.

JINX. But, it's mine.

TAD. I don't care. We're not going into the desert! We're going to San Diego! And you can't open to Treasure box! And THAT'S FINAL! Again.

(Slight pause. They look at each other.)

CORKY. Oh? Hmmm…says who?

TAD. Says me!

CORKY. Oh? Then how to you plan to get to San Diego?

TAD. What do you mean? I'm going in our car.

CORKY. *(holding up and swinging keys)* Ah! Well, strictly speaking, it's not *our* car anymore. It's now *my* car.

TAD. Oh, you wouldn't!

CORKY. Wouldn't what, Tad?

TAD. Make me go to Brawley and miss the wedding.

CORKY. No, not exactly, no.

TAD. I'll be a nervous wreck.

CORKY. Relax, Tad. We'll get there in time. Think of the adventure.

JINX. And I'd really appreciate it…and be terribly indebted to you.

(Pause. They look at each other.)

TAD. *(moaning)* Ugh…Brawley and Babe.

CORKY. Oh, come on, Tad. We can make it. And that tire can make it. We can do it all.

(swinging keys)

Otherwise…

TAD. *(Pause, while he considers his options.)* Okay, okay, you two win. But I'm still against it.

*(**JINX** puts her arms around both **TAD** and **CORKY**)*

JINX. Oh, thank you. Hey, you guys are the greatest! The very best!

CORKY. Yeah, that's true. And, I have the feeling it'll all work out.

JINX. Oh, I hope so.

CORKY. But that's tomorrow. Right now, I'm hungry.

JINX. I know a restaurant nearby. Let's walk.

CORKY. Great idea. Let's go.

*(**CORKY** and **JINX** exit brightly, leaving **TAD** alone.)*

TAD. *(After long moment as he looks reflective, then to self and audience.)* This whole trip is turning into a nightmare.

CORKY. *(off)* Hey, Tad, are you coming?

TAD. *(to self and audience)* We'll never make it, I know we won't.

JINX. *(off, coaxingly)* Taaa-aad? We're waaaiting.

TAD. *(to self and audience)* I can see it all now…disaster in the desert. Well, I guess I'm having romance and adventure – but it's sure no fun.

JINX. *(**JINX** returns and extends her hand, and says affection-ately.)* Come on, Tad. Let's go eat.

*(**TAD** sighs, takes her hand and exits in a cloud of gloom.)*

End of Act One

Intermission

ACT II

(The house lights fade. In the darkness a drum roll and bass drum and ominous music chords to capture hot desert morning. Then, lights come up very brightly with the sound of the motor.It is early morning, about 6 a.m., summer weather in the desert: dry, sunny, and very hot. The sky is not blue – it is white. **CORKY** *is driving and frowning and looking miserable. He is wearing a towel over his head, which is held by a band, making him look like pictures of Lawrence of Arabia.* **JINX** *is in back and dozing with a California map over her head.* **TAD** *is in back sleeping with his head cocked to one side. He has formed a tent-like covering with the blanket to form a shelter.* **JINX** *wakes up, opens one eye and looks around the territory…then closes the eye, shakes her head and moans. Then, she takes the map off of her head and looks at it.)*

JINX. Where are we?

CORKY. Near Palm Springs.

JINX. Whew…! How hot is it?

CORKY. Don't know. The heat affects my what-cha-ma-call-it… – Brain!

JINX. I'm beginning to think this was a crazy idea.

TAD. *(with eyes closed)* That's why *we're* here. Ooooh!

(Moaning in pain, rubbing temples and stretching neck.)

JINX. Poor Tad. I'll put your name in my movie credits.

TAD. Good, 'cause my folks'll take it *out* of their will.

CORKY. *(reading sign)* "PALM SPRINGS 4 MILES." Let's eat breakfast there.

*(Suddenly a **RELIGIOUS-LOOKING PERSON** appears holding out his thumb to hitch a ride. The **RELIGIOUS PERSON** appears to be a nice, pleasant, clean, wholesome person.)*

CORKY. I'll bet this hitchhiker knows someplace good.

(car decelerates)

TAD. Don't stop.

*(**CORKY** stops the car. Car stopping. **TAD** moans.)*

RELIGIOUS PERSON. Morning, Folks. Blessings on you for stopping. I hope you can give a ride to one of God's children on the highway of life.

CORKY. Sure. Hop in.

*(The **RELIGIOUS PERSON** gets in front seat with **CORKY** and **CORKY** takes off again.)*

Know any good restaurants in this area?

RELIGIOUS PERSON. American, Asian, or Mexican?

CORKY. Sure, anything. Look! Here's the Palm Springs exit.

RELIGIOUS PERSON. No, no, don't turn here. Just keep going on...on down the road. I know some better places in Rancho Mirage. Meantime, till we find some place that's suitable, let me share my bag of bagels, and box of raisins with you...with my blessings.

CORKY. Blessings on you, too. *And,* your bagels and raisins.

TAD. *(gloomily)* Yeah...blessings.

RELIGIOUS PERSON. Anyone in the back seat like a bagel?

TAD. Sure. Why not?

CORKY. Where're you headed?

RELIGIOUS PERSON. Uh...to an international religious conference in, uh...Plaster City.

TAD. *Plaster City...?!*

RELIGIOUS PERSON. Uh, yes. After that I'm off to San Juan Capistrano to see the swallows.

CORKY. Sounds like fun.

RELIGIOUS PERSON. Yes. Yes, indeed. Very spiritual.

(Pause. They drive on a short time with everyone looking uncomfortable, but eating.)

CORKY. How much further is it?

RELIGIOUS PERSON. Take this side road here.

CORKY. Side road? You sure?

RELIGIOUS PERSON. Definitely.

*(***CORKY*** *turns the car doubtfully.)*

CORKY. It looks kind of deserted along here.

RELIGIOUS PERSON. It's just the place I've been looking for. *Stop the car!*

CORKY. What…?!

RELIGIOUS PERSON. I said, STOP THIS CAR! I want to get out right here!

CORKY. Here?

RELIGIOUS PERSON. Yes! RIGHT NOW!

CORKY. But this is in the middle of nowhere.

RELIGIOUS PERSON. This is where I'm going! STOP! NOW!

*(***CORKY*** *puts on brakes. Brakes screeching. The car stops. The* **RELIGIOUS PERSON** *reaches over and turns off engine – engine stops – and* **RELIGIOUS PERSON** *takes out keys.)*

CORKY. Hey, you took the keys.

RELIGIOUS PERSON. That's right, sonny. And if you're a good boy, you may get them back.

(The **RELIGIOUS PERSON** *pulls out a gun.)*

Now STICK 'EM UP!

*(***CORKY*** *looks startled and raises his hands.)*

CORKY. Uh, Tad, Jinx. Yoo-hoo.

*(***TAD*** *and* **JINX** *slowly come out from under the blanket and map with their hands up.)*

RELIGIOUS PERSON. Okay, now slowly…give me all your money.

CORKY. Can I put my arms down to reach my pockets?

RELIGIOUS PERSON. Quit stalling, Dumbo!

> (**CORKY** *and* **TAD** *begin to get out their money.*)

> Everybody makes an offering. Open your hearts and wallets. It's for a very worthy cause. Me.

> (*The* **RELIGIOUS PERSON** *passes hat or equivalent and they deposit money or jewelry.*)

JINX. I don't have much money.

RELIGIOUS PERSON. Well then, kiddo, I'll take some of that dime store jewelry you're wearing.

JINX. But this is all I've got.

RELIGIOUS PERSON. Good. Everything is appreciated. And blessings on you one and all.

> (*noting Treasure Box*)

> Whoa! Wait a minute. What's this box?

> (*picks it up*)

JINX/TAD. Oh, nooooo! Don't take that.

RELIGIOUS PERSON. Why not?

JINX. No, please, it's a gift from my father.

RELIGIOUS PERSON. What's in this nicely carved box?

JINX. I don't know. Honest!

CORKY. Me, either.

TAD. But don't open it.

RELIGIOUS PERSON. Why not?

TAD. I'm responsible for it.

> (*The* **RELIGIOUS PERSON** *sets down his gun out of the reach of* **CORKY**, **TAD** *and* **JINX** *in order to examine the box.*)

RELIGIOUS PERSON. Hmmmm. It sounds more valuable than I thought. Let's see now…if I just turn this little latch…I might be able to….

> (*Just then, a grizzled* **OLD PROSPECTOR** *appears from out of nowhere. He carries a shotgun, and moves behind the* **RELIGIOUS PERSON**.)

PROSPECTOR. Whoa there, Stranger! Don't reach for that gun. Put down that Treasure Box and back off.

(*The* **RELIGIOUS PERSON** *puts box down and steps back.*)

Good. Now that shows a nice, friendly spirit.

JINX. He just pretended to be religious. He tried to steal everything from us.

RELIGIOUS PERSON. That was a misunderstanding.

PROSPECTOR. Heh, heh. It sure was.

RELIGIOUS PERSON. Okay, I'm giving back all their jewelry and things. See. And here, Old Timer, take this. It's all I have.

(*handing over moneybag*)

PROSPECTOR. Is this here all you got?

RELIGIOUS PERSON. Yes. Yes. But, it's yours. Just let me get out of here! Please, Old Timer, please!

PROSPECTOR. Okay, you Scalawag! – Now git!

(*The* **RELIGIOUS PERSON** *runs off fearfully.*)

AND DON'T COME BACK!

CORKY. Hey, you saved our lives.

JINX. Wow! And there's even more money than we gave him!

CORKY. Well, don't call him back for a refund.

TAD. Say, who are you?

PROSPECTOR. Allow me to introduce myself…I'm E.L. Partch, prospector.

JINX. Oh, my Gosh! Dad's old friend, "Spit" Partch!

PROSPECTOR. That's right, Jinxie. I remember you from when you tagged along after your daddy. How you doin', Honey?

JINX. Fine now, thanks to you. And this is Corky and Tad.

SPIT. Howdy, fellows.

TAD & CORKY. Hi, Mr. Partch.

SPIT. Just call me "Spit."

(*spitting*)

Bullseye! Whatcha all doin' out here in the desert?

JINX. Lookin' for my Dad.

SPIT. Stormy? Oh, dear, oh dear! I guess you didn't hear.

JINX. What? What happened?

SPIT. Well, I hate to tell you like this. But, old Stormy…he went to the great rodeo in the sky.

JINX. Oh, no!

(**CORKY** *glances up.*)

SPIT. Yep. Stormy died about five days ago. Buried near the Salton Sea at a place called Mecca.

JINX. "Mecca…?"

SPIT. Yep, and you just missed the funeral. Look, I got a postcard here from a Mexican friend that drew a picture of his grave marker. See, there's the epitaph.

JINX. (*reading*) "Stormy O'Brien, King of Rodeo, Age 49." Oh, no! And that's all. Poor dad.

SPIT. No. He had a full life. Stormy always said, "Life's like a bucking bronco…You gotta hold on tight, and ride full blast till the buzzer."

CORKY. He was quite a philosopher.

SPIT. Yep, he figured: "You gotta get a laugh outa life, or it ain't worth livin'."

CORKY. (*nodding toward* **TAD**) Now that's true. Hear that, Tad?

SPIT. You woulda liked Stormy. He had a devilish sense of humor. Always playin' practical jokes on people.

JINX. How did he die?

SPIT. Well, when he wasn't on the rodeo circuit, he did a lotta work in the cowboy movies.

JINX. What kind of cowboy movies? Was he an actor?

SPIT. More of a stunt man. He didn't mind being an honest stunt man, but he didn't want to be no phony actor playin' no phony cowboy. No bang-bang fall dead stuff. So he went right on being a stunt man.

JINX. What kind of stunts?

SPIT. Did all kinds of dangerous tricks. Some real wild stuff…jumping on runaway horses, leaping horses over chasms, turning over stagecoaches, chariot races and crashes all over! Stuff like that. A real daredevil!

JINX. Did he ever get hurt?

SPIT. Lots o' times. Always covered with bruises. Broke a lot of bones.

JINX. You mean, he died in some stunt man accident?

SPIT. Not exactly. He got into trouble 'cause he was always looking for something new and different…and he loved adventure. But nothing real bad happened till about six months ago when he did a crazy stunt for a Mexican film company. He played a bullfighter in Mexicali, Mexico.

JINX. I didn't know he spoke Spanish.

SPIT. He didn't. But he dyed his red hair and mustache all black. And, he looked great in the outfit. But he was terrible in the bullring. No skill at all. And the bull knew it. But Stormy fought on sheer guts. Ended up getting gored three times.

JINX. Oh, poor Dad! And that's how he died?

SPIT. Don't rightly know. But, after that he had a hard time ridin' horses, an' sittin' down.

(He spits.)

But the worst part of this story is he died without ever making the kind of western cowboy movies he was always dreamin' about.

JINX. Oh, that's so sad.

SPIT. Yep. Stormy had a dream of makin' his own cowboy westerns. And, he figured if he couldn't make 'em the way he wanted to, he might as well be dead.

JINX. I wish I could have been there.

SPIT. Yep, me too. 'Cause everybody's got a dream.

(He spits.)

Well, friends, I gotta go check on some gold in them hills over there 'fore it gets too hot.

TAD. It's already too hot.

SPIT. People keep tellin' me things'll get better, so I'm still waitin'. And I don't like to let one day pass without lookin' for some treasure in my life. Glad to meet you fellas. Good seein' you again, Jinx. You kids have some fun, and lots of romance and adventure, 'cause you only go 'round once in this merry-go-round. So, long!

(He spits.)

Bulls-eye!

*(**SPIT** walks off playing the harmonica. As he walks toward the morning sun, he "dissolves" into the hot desert landscape. **CORKY**, **TAD** and **JINX** stare after him in awe and amazement.)*

TAD. Hey, look, he's gone….! He just evaporated into the desert!

CORKY. Yeah, like a mirage.

JINX. Oooooh, that's spooky. I feel so strange about this whole thing. I saw the postcard, so I guess Dad is really dead, but…maybe I should go over and…

TAD. Nothing we can do about it now! And, we're running really late. I'll drive. Let's go!

*(They all get in the car with **TAD** driving. Car starting rapidly as they continue on their journey. TIME TRAVEL, SOUND MUSIC starts as Lights fade to half. After a few moments the lights come up to full again.It is some time later. They are traveling south on Highway 86 near the Salton Sea. **JINX** is in back looking depressed and staring off dreamily. **CORKY** is holding map and reading highway signs.)*

CORKY. Look, Tad, the Salton Sea. We're getting close to where old what's-her-name from Borrego Springs runs the Desert Oasis Gas Station. We could stop there to get something to eat.

TAD. No, no. I don't want to see Babe.

CORKY. I always thought she was a true American original with her pigtails and bib overalls. We could just get gas. You could hide in the trunk.

TAD. NO!

JINX. Why don't you want to see her?

TAD. Well…one night…three years ago…I took her to a dance in Calexico. She hummed and sang in my ear until I couldn't stand it anymore. So, I ditched her.

CORKY. He thinks she'll never forgive him.

TAD. Poor Babe. She'll probably live and die in Borrego Springs.

(*Just then, the car begins to chug, sputter and lurch.*)

Oh, no! Now what?

CORKY. Sounds like the Wild Goose is having a nervous breakdown.

(*The car comes to a jerky stop.* **TAD** *moans.*)

JINX. You mean we'll have to walk?

CORKY. No, no, Tad'll take a look at the whatcha-ma-callit – engine, and see what's wrong.

TAD. We're out of gas. *(to **CORKY**)* I thought you took care of the gas.

CORKY. Gosh, Tad, I guess it must have evaporated…or something

TAD. Ooooh, it's hopeless. We'll never get to the wedding on time.

JINX. You could go back to Beverly's gas station.

TAD. Not me.

JINX. Why not? You're familiar with the desert…

CORKY. Not to mention Babe. And you know the technical language for what the car needs.

TAD. It's called gas. And it's your car.

CORKY. Well, I'm not going.

TAD. Ummmm. *(beat)* Okay, okay. Maybe she won't remember me.

(**TAD** *starts to leave.*)

JINX. *(calling after)* Don't worry, Tad. We'll keep an eye on everything.

(TAD grumbles, "All right," and leaves. A pause. JINX and CORKY are alone. They look around for a moment. Pause.)

JINX. Oh, Corky, this whole experience is so unreal. I don't know what to believe. Is Dad really dead? I don't know. Maybe. The only thing that seems to be left… out of this whole trip…is my Treasure Box. Maybe I could find out something more about Dad if I could just open it. I don't know. Maybe it could answer some questions.

CORKY. Could be.

JINX. Hmmmm…I wonder…what could possibly be in here?

(CORKY shrugs. Pause.)

Corky, you think maybe if I…I mean, I know I shouldn't…But…What do you think?

CORKY. I think maybe yes.

JINX. You really think I should?

CORKY. I don't see why not.

JINX. Well, okay, then…

(She reaches to open the box. TAD suddenly reappears.)

TAD. STOP RIGHT THERE!

(They jump in surprise.)

Don't you dare open that box!

JINX. OH! You scared me!

TAD. You were about to open that box, weren't you?

JINX. No, no, I wasn't. We were just talking. And I was admiring it.

TAD. *(reaching for Treasure Box)* In fact, since I'm responsible for guarding this Treasure Box I better take it with me.

JINX. No, don't. Please, Tad, it's perfectly safe here with us. If you take it with you, it's just going to take a lot longer. You'll never make it both ways in the heat.

CORKY. That's right. You go on, Tad. You can trust us.

(Pause. He looks at them suspiciously. **CORKY** *and* **JINX** *nod and smile.* **TAD** *looks how far he may have to go and sighs.)*

TAD. Ummmm, well, okay. Back shortly.

*(***TAD*** *leaves again. Pause again. They watch* **TAD** *walk away.)*

JINX. Well, of course, I know I promised, and I know I shouldn't. But.. *(beat)* Oh! I don't know if I can control my curiosity much longer. I'm getting so excited. What if I opened it?

CORKY. They said it could release all the sins of the world.

JINX. Yeah! Wow! That's right. That would be some kind of experience, wouldn't it?

JINX. OH! Look at these hideous little dancing figures on the box...all sort of moldy moss green. OH!

(harp chords)

CORKY. What?

JINX. The little carved figures just moved!

CORKY. Moved...?

JINX. I was just looking at them, and they moved.

(more harp chords)

OH! Listen. Did you hear that?

CORKY. What?

JINX. It was like harp chords or small voices crying out. It sounded like, "Let me out! Let me out!"

(more harp chords)

CORKY. Oh, yeah! Wow, that's weird.

JINX. Oh, Corky, I know I promised and I know it's forbidden...but...if my dad's really dead...and my Uncle Herman and Tad are not here to know...then, I don't see what harm it could do to open the box. Do you?

CORKY. Well no, but what if you opened it, and found out more than you wanted to know?

JINX. Oh, wouldn't that be exciting? Think about it... releasing all the mysteries of life. Oh, Corky, I'm so curious and excited it gives me goose pimples. And I don't think I can control my curiosity much longer. Tell me to open it.

CORKY. Well, Wow! What can a red-blooded guy say?

JINX. Corky! – TELL ME!

CORKY. OPEN IT!

JINX. Oh, yes, yes!

CORKY. Slowly now. Very slowly.

> *(Harp chords with a tremolo of excitement that reflects* **JINX**' *excitement as she slowly opens the Treasure Box and looks in. As she does so, everything is enveloped in a green light!)*

JINX. Oooooh, MY! It's all musty.

> *(She sneezes.)*

What a strange collection. Ooooh! A little green bug flew out!

CORKY. Look, here's an old rodeo flyer...all burned around the edges...

JINX. With Stormy's name at the top...

CORKY. *(reading flyer)* "King of the California Rodeos."

JINX. And the belt buckle with S.O.B. on it, just like Mom said. And look at this turquoise ring. It says "CURIOS-ITY" inside.

> *(She puts it on. Harp chords.)*

CORKY. And here's a silver spur...just like your Uncle Herman's Post Office. With the word "HOPE" carved on the side.

> *(pricking his finger)*

OW! Ooooh, that hurts!

JINX. *(suddenly sad)* Oh, Corky, that's all there is, and it's all just leftover junk. I'll never get to talk to my dad again, and I don't know any more than I did before. What am I going to do?

CORKY. Don't know. I'm sorry.

JINX. Here we are in the middle of the California desert in a broken down car with a box of leftover junk. You and Tad are going to miss Sally's wedding. And it's all my fault.

CORKY. Well…It was an adventure.

JINX. Oh, Corky, I botched the whole thing. I feel miserable and guilty. Will you and Tad ever forgive me?

CORKY. I will. 'Cause I still like you, anyway. A lot.

JINX. I like you, too, Corky. Oh, look…on the inside of the lid…an old cracked mirror.

(They put their heads together and look at themselves in the mirror. Suddenly, a strong green light comes over them. The harp chords make weird sounds that suggest something that is not quite earthly, but somewhat romantic and sexy.)

CORKY. How do we look?

JINX. Terrible. We're all green and distorted and ugly. OH! I suddenly feel devilish, and sexy and evil! Oooohhh!

CORKY. Yeah, me, too. Maybe we're both dizzy from the sun.

JINX. I don't think so.

CORKY. I don't either.

JINX. I think it's something else.

CORKY. I do, too.

JINX. What do you think we ought to do about it?

CORKY. As a good friend of yours, I think we ought to make the most of a miserable situation.

JINX. *(wickedly)* Me, too. And maybe we can do something that's wicked and evil and forbidden. Wouldn't that be exciting?

CORKY. Yeahhhh…I'll say.

*(**CORKY** smiles and nods. He raises the blanket to make a tent and cover themselves. The soft sound of harp chords grows into weird, space-like sounds as they lower the blanket.)*

(Lights fade on area of car and cross fade to reveal the stage area where the Desert Oasis Gas Station is located. It's a short time later. **TAD** *cautiously enters. No one appears to be there.)*

TAD. *(looking around hesitantly)* Hello…? Anybody here?

(After a moment, **BEVERLY "BABE" BORDEN** *appears. She is the same age as* **TAD***…mid-to-late 20s. She's changed from* **TAD***'s description of an innocent, awkward, gauche, tomboy type of girl to her present warm, hearty, saucy, bouncy, no-nonsense, self-confident young woman who is in control.)*

BEVERLY. Hey, hey! Is that really you, Tad Miller? I never expected to see you again.

TAD. Oh, hi, Beverly.

BEVERLY. I mean, not after the way you deserted me at that dance in Calexico.

TAD. Oh, yeah. I see you haven't forgotten. I'm sorry about that.

BEVERLY. No need to apologize, old buddy. Forget it. I have. Fact is, I would have deserted the old me, too. What're you doing around these parts? Don't tell me you were just driving by.

TAD. Actually, we were, uh…just driving by…on the way to my sister's wedding. And we ran out of gas.

BEVERLY. I figured it wasn't a social call. I heard your sister Sally is getting married in San Diego.

TAD. Yeah. I'm on the way to the wedding, but everything keeps going wrong.

BEVERLY. Listen, old buddy, I was going to ask you a favor for old times' sake.

TAD. What's that?

BEVERLY. Come on, we'll catch up and I'll tell you all about it while I'm getting your gas.

(The lights fade on Beverly's area and again come up on the car. It's a little while later. **CORKY** *and* **JINX** *are still in the car under the blanket. From under the blanket*

come the sounds of gentle sighs, moans, and soft giggles. The blanket moves slightly and gently. After a moment, **TAD** *appears from upstage looking totally exhausted and hot as he slowly trudges toward the car with a container of gas.)*

*(***BEVERLY*** *or "Babe" walks behind with a small suitcase. As* **TAD** *approaches the car, he notices the tent-like arrangement that covers* **CORKY** *and* **JINX.** **TAD** *looks at it, then listens disgustedly to the following sexy conversation between* **CORKY** *and* **JINX** *that comes from under the blanket.* **BABE** *listens with amusement.)*

JINX. *(unseen)* Cor-ky…?

CORKY. *(unseen)* Yeah, Jinx-ie?

JINX. *(unseen)* You awake…?

CORKY. *(unseen)* Yeah. I was just dozing and dreaming.

JINX. *(unseen)* What're you dreaming about?

CORKY. *(unseen)* Was dreaming about you.

JINX. *(unseen)* Me…?

CORKY. *(unseen)* Ummmm…huh.

JINX. *(unseen)* And I was dreaming about you, too.

CORKY. *(unseen)* What were you dreaming about me?

JINX. *(unseen)* It was kind of romantic.

CORKY. *(unseen)* Yeah, me, too you.

(The sound of smacking kisses and they giggle and **TAD** *looks thoroughly disgusted. He finally can't stand it anymore, so he moves over and pulls off the blanket.* **CORKY** *and* **JINX** *look giddy and lazy and silly.* **JINX** *speaks in a breathy romantic manner.)*

JINX. Oh, hiiii there, Tad-dy.

*(***CORKY*** *waves giddily with his fingers.)*

TAD. WHAT…ARE…YOU…TWO…DOING!?

CORKY. OOoooh, nothing much really.

(They both giggle.)

TAD. I leave for thirty minutes, and when I get back I find you two playing "mousy" again.

CORKY & JINX. Yeah, FUN!

(They nod and giggle.)

TAD. And look, *you've opened the box!*

CORKY. Yeah, I know.

JINX. We couldn't resist.

*(**CORKY** and **JINX** giggle throughout the next few lines.)*

TAD. *How could you two do that?*

CORKY. Easy. Nothing to it.

JINX. I just turned the latch, and bingo, it opened.

CORKY. And right after that we fell apart.

JINX. Right! – Came all unglued!

CORKY. Yeeeeeeah! It was soooo neat!

(They giggle giddily.)

TAD. And look what you've done! RELEASED ALL THE SINS OF THE WORLD.

CORKY. Tad, buddy, you name the sin, and we've got it! WHOOOEEE!

*(**CORKY** and **JINX** giggle, then hug and kiss each other somewhat wildly.)*

TAD. OH, NO! LAZY, LUST, PASSION, DECADENCE! AGH! That's disgusting!

JINX. Well, Taddy, it isn't easy to be decadent.

CORKY. No. You have to work at it. Ha!

JINX. And, look at YOU! – ENVIOUS AND ANGRY!

TAD. *(angrily)* I'm NOT envious! And I'm not ANGRY either! Just because I promised your Uncle Herman, and you two promised me not to open the Treasure Box, and you opened it, anyway, and we all broke our promises is no reason for me to be *angry!* And, I'm NOT ANGRY! – I'M NOT!

JINX. *(proudly)* Well, why should *we* have to keep a silly promise like that?

TAD. And PRIDE! I suppose you're also guilty of *greed* and *gluttony!*

JINX. I'm not sure about Greed.

CORKY. But, I…LOVE…GLUTTONY!

(*They laugh and giggle again.*)

TAD. *That's enough*! You've got to get control of yourselves. I'm putting an end to this right now. Here, give me that Box!

(**TAD** *grabs the treasure box and closes the lid firmly with a thud! As he does so, it's as if this "breaks the spell" and harp chords momentarily fill the air, and the pool of green light begins to fade and natural light of the hot desert returns and harp chords fade. There is a long pause as they look at each other and everyone's demeanor returns to a more normal level.*)

JINX. Listen, Tad, don't be such a fuddy-duddy! Before we opened the box, I was going to apologize for all the trouble I caused you. But now it doesn't seem to matter.

(*They all pause thoughtfully. Then, suddenly out of the silence,* **BEVERLY** *speaks.*)

BEVERLY. Hey, Tad, buddy, are you gonna put gas in this old buggy or not?

TAD. What? Oh, yeah. Uh…this is Beverly.

JINX/CORKY. (*together*) Hi, Beverly.

BEVERLY. Just call me "Babe."

JINX. Are you the person Tad deserted at a dance?

BABE. That's me. But the truth is, I'm glad he did, 'cause I couldn't stand him whistling and singing in my ear.

(**CORKY** *and* **JINX** *smirk and glance at* **TAD** *who looks embarrassed at this revelation.*)

TAD. Babe generously gave us some free gas 'cause our car doesn't operate very well on "Empty."

BABE. In the old days when Tad's car stalled on "Empty," he was *more* than able to operate. In fact, when the car stalled, Tad moved a whole lot faster. But those were the old days. The new me is a horse of another ballgame. I'm a bit older, and a lot wiser and sassier since Tad deserted me at that dance in Calexico.

TAD. She'll never forgive me.

JINX. *(noting suitcase)* Are you joining us?

BABE. Yeah, Terrible Tad agreed to take me to San Diego.

TAD. Her folks just died, and left her a big uranium mine up near Borrego Springs.

BABE. So, Tad volunteered to take me as far as San Diego to start a new life.

CORKY. Very thoughtful of Tad.

JINX. By the way, since you're from around here, did you ever know a guy named Stormy O'Brien?

BABE. Oh, yeah! We all did. Is he a friend of yours?

JINX. Something like that.

BABE. Nobody was neutral. He had lots of charm…bigger than life…with all his rodeoin', guitar-playin', and story telling. Acted like a movie star. He flirted with all of us. Why?

JINX. That's my dad.

BABE. Oh, well then there was the other side. When my folks died, he consoled me a lot. He always called me "Babe."

JINX. Where is he now?

BABE. Um, don't know exactly.

CORKY. We just heard Stormy was dead.

BABE. *(laughing heartily)* Stormy…dead?! Hah! Naw, don't you believe it! In March he won the Cattle Call Rodeo in Brawley. Best all-around cowboy. He was 'round my place all the time eating and drinking, and charging everything. Then, he disappeared without paying. But he's not dead. Not Stormy.

JINX. Are you sure?

BABE. Listen, when Stormy dies, Gabriel will blow his horn, and cowboys will ride across the sky. So, he's not dead. Not by a long shot! Take my word for it.

JINX. Could he still be in Brawley?

BABE. Naw. He was. But he's gone by now.

TAD. Okay. We're all gassed up. I'll drive.

CORKY. Why you?

TAD. I won the bet.

CORKY. What bet?

TAD. You tempted Jinx in opening that box and letting out all those evil spirits. So, I get the car back.

CORKY. Half the car.

TAD. All right…half the car.

CORKY. The back half.

TAD. Back half, front half. What difference does it make?

CORKY. If it makes no difference, then I'll take the engine, and you get the rear end, tail pipe and the back tire that could explode at any moment.

TAD. Okay, okay, whatever. Everybody in?

ALL. We're in!

TAD. Then, we're off!

BABE. *San Diego here we come!*

TAD. *(with a resigned sigh)* Oh, I hope so!

> *(**TAD** starts motor, and again takes off to san diego. The lights are lowered to half briefly as we hear "TIME/ TRAVEL – SOUND/MUSIC" to indicate the passage of time to a new place.)*
>
> *(After a few moments the lights come up again to full and they are now on a freeway in the San Diego area. It is about 11:45 Sunday morning. **TAD** is driving and **BABE** is in front with him looking at a map. **CORKY** is in the back with **JINX**. **JINX** appears thoughtful for a moment then speaks. **TAD** checks his watch.)*

TAD. Eleven forty five and we're almost there. Just as long as I make it by noon, I'll be okay.

JINX. You know, there are still some things that baffle me. If Stormy's a winner, and a money maker, but is still in debt to Uncle Herman, owes my Mom back alimony, and even owes Babe for groceries…– Where'd all the money go?

CORKY. Yeah. And he seemed to have some sort of love-hate relationship with the movies.

JINX. But most of all…is he really dead, or isn't he? And if he's alive, where is he? I just don't know where I go from here or what I do next.

CORKY. Let's worry about it after the wedding.

BABE. *(with map)* Coming into San Diego!

TAD. Finally! I never thought we'd make it, but here we are.

BABE. Just goes to show…Never give up hope.

TAD. I still think we're going to be late.

BABE. Maybe we can get there for the reception.

TAD. More likely the honeymoon.

CORKY. That sounds good to me. I'll bring my camera.

BABE. Where's the wedding?

TAD. *(looking around)* Someplace here in the Gaslight District?

> *(The lights come up slowly on the whole stage. There is a street area with low wall at the end.)*

BABE. There's no one around.

TAD. They've blocked off all the streets.

BABE. Let's stop here by the Murphy's OK Feed Store.

> *(Car stopping. Suddenly, gunshot #1 from offstage.)*

JINX. What's that…?!

TAD. Somebody's shooting at somebody. GET DOWN!

> *(**TAD**, **BABE** and **JINX** crouch down in the car. **CORKY** looks around innocently.)*

CORKY. Maybe Sally's having a shotgun wedding.

TAD. Not my sister Sally!

BABE. That's not a shotgun. That's a six-shooter.

> *(Gunshot #2 from offstage.)*

TAD. DUCK! BABE! DUCK!

> *(They duck again. Gunshot #3 from offstage.)*

CORKY. *(faking being shot)* UGH! They got me!

> *(falling in **JINX**'s arms)*

JINX & TAD. COR-KY…!!

JINX. *(with concern)* Where'd they hit you?

CORKY. Ughhhh…! I don't know.

> *(last gasping breath)*

> Jinx…Jinx, I…I love you. Ugh! Ugh!

> *(flopping in* **JINX**' *arms)*

JINX. *(with great concern)* COR-KY!

> *(Beat. She realizes he's play-acting.)*

> OH! You're NOT SHOT!

CORKY. I know. But I've always wanted to die magnificently in a woman's arms…like they do in the movies. Aghhhhh!

> *(His head flops again…as if "dead.")*

JINX. *(pushing him away…disgustedly)* COR-KY!! – DON'T DO THAT TO ME!!

> *(**TAD** peeks up, points to **CORKY**, and calls to people shooting guns.)*

TAD. Here he is! – SHOOT HIM!

> *(Gunshot # 4 from offstage.)*

JINX & BABE & CORKY. TAD….!! DUCK!

> *(Just then, a hat appears from behind the low wall at one end of the street area, and it is held up by a stick with a model's head or a mask in front. Simultaneously, on the other side of the stage, A **YOUNG WOMAN** emerges in front of **THE VILLAIN**, who has her in a choke hold. She is tied, somewhat gagged and looking fearful as they move cautiously on stage. They slowly cross in front of the car. Note: If it's a particularly small stage this part could be played in the audience area.)*

SALLY. *(letting out a muffled sound)* HELP! HEEEEEELLLLLP!!

> *(**CORKY**, **TAD**, **JINX** and **BABE** look up and see the **YOUNG WOMAN** flailing. **TAD** points to **YOUNG WOMAN**.)*

TAD. *(stage whisper)* Look! It's SALLY!

SALLY. SAAAAAAVE ME!

TAD. Oh, no! She's in danger!

>   *(rising up in car slightly)*

>   LET GO OF MY SISTER!

>   (**THE VILLAIN** *shoots gunshot # 5 toward the hat.*)

BABE. DUCK, TAD! DUCK!

>   (**TAD** *ducks.*)

SALLY. HEEELLLLPPP!

VOICE OF STORMY. *(offstage left from behind the wall)* DON'T HURT THAT GIRL!

JINX. OH! – Hear that! That's my Dad's voice!

TAD. That's Stormy O'Brien…?

JINX. Yes! He's alive!

BABE. I told you he wasn't dead.

VOICE OF STORMY. *(off)* RELEASE THAT GIRL!

>   *(gunshot #6)*

THE VILLAIN. Then, gimme the bag of gold coins!

VOICE OF STORMY. *(off)* Okay. Here it is.

>   *(Still unseen, **STORMY** throws a small old-style pouch on the ground downstage that makes up the street.)*

>   Come get them.

>   (**THE VILLAIN** *cautiously moves forward from one side of the stage to other with* **SALLY** *in front of him – using her as a shield – and his arm around her neck in a chokehold style.)*

THE VILLAIN. *Don't move!* And don't do anything funny!

VOICE OF STORMY. *(off, unseen)* Okay! I'm staying right here, till you pick up the money, and release the girl. And I promise not to do anything funny.

>   *(As **THE VILLAIN** cautiously moves forward, he thinks that seeing **STORMY**'s hat on the wall means that **STORMY** is still behind the wall. But, **STORMY** appears*

upstage. **THE VILLAIN** *doesn't see* **STORMY** *move stealthily along the upstage plane to above the car, then along the side of the car to the backside of the where* **THE VILLAIN** *is. As* **STORMY** *is seen by* **JINX** *in the car, she gasps, and* **STORMY** *motions with his finger to his lips for her to be quiet. As* **THE VILLAIN** *gets to the money-bag, he lets go of* **SALLY** *and moves forward and as he kneels down greedily for the money he sets down his gun. As he leans back on his haunches to open the moneybag* **STORMY** *moves in quickly and with index finger puts it in* **THE VILLAIN**'*s back.)*

STORMY. Don't move or I'll shoot.

*(***THE VILLAIN*** raises his arms, but as he does so glances over his shoulder and sees that* **STORMY** *is only pointing his finger and has no gun.)*

VILLAIN. Ha! You don't have a gun.

(He reaches for his gun again picks it up again, and aims it at **STORMY***.)*

But I do!

(Meanwhile, as he does so, **SALLY** *quickly picks up* **STORMY**'*s real gun.)*

So, don't move or I'll shoot!

STORMY. Go ahead. It won't do you any good. You've already fired six shots. It's empty.

*(***THE VILLAIN*** pulls the trigger of the gun and it clicks.)*

But Sally Lou has my gun and she doesn't mind using it.

SALLY. And I'm not being funny!

THE VILLAIN. Okay, Stormy O'Brien. You and Sally Lou have done it again. I surrender.

STORMY. *(calling off into the wings)* Okay, Sheriff, here he is. Get him out of our lives.

*(***THE VILLAIN*** slowly walks off with head down.)*

Sally Lou! – MY HEROINE!

SALLY. STORMY O'BRIEN – MY HERO.

> (**SALLY** *rushes into* **STORMY**'*s arms looking at him with an idolizing gaze. They both look front with proud smiles and hold the pose a moment like a satire of an old style romantic operetta.*)

JINX. *(Intense whisper. In awe.)* Stormy rescued Sally!

TAD. *(intense whisper)* Thank God she's safe!

> (*Then,* **STORMY** *calls out into audience area.*)

STORMY. CUT!

JINX. *(rising in the car)* "Cut…?" Did he say "Cut…?"

STORMY. Okay! – That it! That's a wrap. WRAP IT UP!

JINX. "Wrap it up?"

CORKY. That's movie talk.

BABE. That's right. They finished the movie.

JINX & TAD. What movie?

STORMY. *(calling to unseen crew)* Okay, Men, pack up the stuff, and put it all in the van. Here. Let me help you.

> (*He exits.*)

SALLY. *(to people in car)* Hey, guys, you can come out now. We're all through. Tad, Corky hi!

> (*The greetings that follow overlap.*)

TAD. Sally! Gee, you're safe.

SALLY. Oh, Tad. I was never in danger.

TAD. I was. I was almost shot.

SALLY. No, you weren't. Those weren't real bullets.

TAD. No?

SALLY. No. Movie people never use real bullets.

TAD. "Movie people?" *What's going on here?!*

SALLY. We're making a movie.

JINX. What movie?

TAD. What about the wedding?

SALLY. It's all over.

TAD. All over! But I got here before noon. I made it just in time for the wedding.

SALLY. No, you didn't. I'm married. I got married this morning at sunrise. And, I said, "I do"…just as the sun came up over Murphy's OK Feed Store.

TAD. But I thought you were getting married at noon.

SALLY. We changed it. I mean, I changed it.

TAD. Again?

SALLY. Yes. When Corky called me on Friday night I told him we changed the time of the wedding to sunrise so we could spend the morning finishing the film.

(faked surprise)

Didn't Corky tell you?

TAD. *Corky? No, he didn't!*

CORKY. It must have slipped my mind.

TAD. Oh, no it didn't. You planned this whole thing… just so I'd be late. You drove me crazy with all those detours? *And you did all that on purpose!* And you made me miss the whole wedding.

CORKY. Easy now, Tad. If we'd been here at sunrise we would have missed the whole California odyssey…with all the romance, adventure and fun.

TAD. It wasn't fun for me being late.

CORKY. But, you'll have to admit it was a great trip.

TAD. Not for me it wasn't. I had an upset stomach and a headache the whole time. And, I didn't have a chance to give my sister away to the groom. But, hey, if you're married, where's Sam Simpson?

SALLY. Oh, I didn't marry Sam.

TAD. He jilted you?

SALLY. No.

CORKY. You jilted him?

SALLY. No. Well, yes, sort of.

TAD. What do you mean, "sort of?"

SALLY. I never really wanted to marry an *insurance salesman.* And, once I got to know Sam, he was really *boring*! Actually, I fell in love with someone else.

TAD. Then, who did you marry?

(**STORMY** *returns.*)

STORMY. HEEEEY, JINXIEEEE….!

JINX. DAD! HI!

STORMY. HOWDY, HONEY!

(**STORMY** *picks* **JINX** *up and swings her around in the air, puts her down and hugs her.*)

JINX. YOU OKAY?

STORMY. Never been better! And you look great, little lady! And it's mighty good to see you again! Howdy, Babe. Lookin' good there.

BABE. So, are you, Stormy.

JINX. Will someone please to tell me – WHAT'S GOING ON HERE? Is this one of your practical jokes?

STORMY. Well, Jinx, honey, you started this whole thing.

JINX. *I did…?*

STORMY. Yep, when you sent your cowboy story to my old friend, Johnny Youngblood, he sent it to me. And right away I liked it. So, I told him if he'd produce the movie, and let you write the script, and let me cast all my friends, then, I'd be willing to play the lead, and back it financially.

BABE. He always gets the lead.

JINX. Well, that explains what happened to all the money you owe people. It went into your movie.

(*indignantly*)

But this wasn't *my* movie. What about my script the one I've been working on?

STORMY. Your movie is next, honey. And I'm looking forward to working on it with you and filling you in some details you may not know about me.

BABE. And I'll bet there are plenty.

JINX. But I still don't understand everything. I mean, how did Corky, Tad and I get involved.

STORMY. That was Sally's idea. She dreamed up that part so you'd have more to write about in our next movie called *"California Odyssey."* It's about two guys who pick up a girl looking for her father.

JINX. I thought that was fate.

STORMY. Not really. I arranged for the band…

JINX. The Western Saints.

STORMY. Right…to leave you off at the Summit on Highway 17…

JINX. They didn't "leave me off" – they ditched me. But…

SALLY. Then, I told Corky to be on the lookout for you.

TAD & JINX. *Corky?!*

CORKY. Yep, and there she was, just as planned.

STORMY. After that I contacted my Carnival friends in Santa Cruz, then talked to Lita and Herman and finally convinced Margo to go along with the whole idea. Margo took a little more convincing. But they all agreed so you could have the kind of experience and great adventures to help you write your wonderful movie.

SALLY. Everybody had a role to play.

JINX. Gosh! Well, that explains almost everything till we went into the desert. We had some pretty unreal experiences. And I just don't understand all the things that happened to us.

STORMY. Like what, honey?

JINX. Well, we had a really scary adventure when we almost got robbed!

STORMY. Robbed?

JINX. Yeah. And I was really frightened. But thanks to your old friend, Spit Partch, he saved us from some phony religious person.

STORMY. You saw Spit Partch?

JINX. Yeah, just outside Rancho Mirage.

STORMY. Huh! Well, people keep telling me they see him around those parts. The only thing is…Spit died 7 years ago.

JINX. He died…?

STORMY. Yep, sure did. After he spent his whole lifetime looking for gold, he finally hit it big…found lots of gold out there. But then, some corporation came along and stole it from him. It broke his heart. He lost his spirit for living. He was never the same again.

JINX. But we saw him…bigger than life. Didn't we guys?

TAD. I think so.

CORKY. I saw him for sure. I know I did.

STORMY. Yeah, well, he's dead. Buried somewhere around those parts. I think it was Mecca maybe. But I keep hearing stories how he still shows up every so often and helps travelers whenever they're in trouble. Don't know what to make of it.

JINX. But Dad, then how do you explain all the magic powers of the Treasure Box?

STORMY. Magic…?

CORKY. Maybe it wasn't magic, but there was something going on out there. Wow!

JINX. There certainly was.

STORMY. Jinx, Honey, I think you felt all those secret magical powers of love and romance because you hoped and believed they could happen.

JINX. You mean, I imagined the whole experience and there was no magic in the Treasure Box? It was all in my mind?

STORMY. I truly believe that's what happened. You know, sometimes things happen in people's lives you just can't explain. Call it fate or love or whatever…It's just part of the myth of the desert. And, you just have to accept it, and move on.

JINX. Well, then, I guess that's what we'll do.

CORKY. Yeah. Sounds good to me.

JINX. And, if it hadn't been for fate to run out of gas when we did, Tad wouldn't have gotten to know Babe again.

BABE. That wasn't fate, Kiddo. Corky didn't fill the tank, and we figured you'd run out of gas just about the time you did.

TAD. You mean, you were in on it, too?

BABE. You bet. Right from the start.

JINX. Well, how about that! Tad, I guess everybody knew but us.

TAD. Yeah. And I hate being left out all the time.

BABE. But when they make the picture you'll be one of the stars of *California Odyssey.*

TAD. *(pouting)* I don't want to be a star. I just wanted to… *(pause)*

BABE. What…?

TAD. Get to the wedding on time…and give away my sister to the groom. And it's all over.

SALLY. Tad, honey, when it got right down to it, I couldn't see my little brother "giving me away" to anybody.

TAD. But, if you didn't marry Sam Simpson, who did you marry? And where is he?

SALLY. Haven't you figured it out by now? Everybody else has… – It's Stormy O'Brien.

TAD & JINX. STORMY O'BRIEN…! MY DAD?!

STORMY. That's right, Folks.

SALLY. I couldn't help myself. I love him. I love the man. He's the only man I've ever really loved. Right, Stormy?

STORMY. That's right, honey.

JINX. But how'd you two ever meet?

SALLY. Oh, it was years ago. At the rodeo…when I was a little girl…I just turned 13. Stormy won everything. And in his excitement, he rode over to the crowd… reached into the front row…and lifted me onto his horse and rode around waving at all the people. I loved it. And I've loved Stormy ever since. What else can I say?

STORMY. That's right. Me, too, honey.

TAD. I can't believe this.

STORMY. You better believe it, Tad, 'cause, I'm gonna be around for a mighty long time as your brother-in-law.

TAD. Stormy is my brother-in-law? How about that!

JINX. Then, you're my uncle...!

TAD. And you're my niece...!

JINX. Then, that means that...Sally is my stepmother.

> *(Both* **JINX** *and* **TAD** *laugh at the ridiculousness.)*

STORMY. And that makes us all *one big happy family*! And that's the way I like it!

TAD. Yeah, but...we drove all this way, and we still missed the whole wedding?

SALLY. That's okay. We're going to have the reception tomorrow night in San Francisco.

JINX. *San Francisco!*

TAD. *Tomorrow night!*

STORMY. Right. At the Palace of Fine Arts. And we're going to show the uncut film of the movie we just made.

SALLY. *(checking watch)* Oh, my Gosh! Come on, Stormy! We've got to catch our charter flight or we'll be late!

STORMY. Right. See you all in the Bay Area. Bye!

> *(Chattering excitedly, they all exit.)*

TAD. Hey, but...But we can't...!

> *(The four are left alone and stunned for a moment.)*

CORKY. *(directly to audience)* No one will ever believe this story.

> *(Then, a long pause and* **JINX** *rallies.)*

JINX. Okay! So, when do *we* leave for San Francisco?

CORKY. Why not now? Right now!

JINX. Good! I can hardly wait.

BABE. I'm ready.

CORKY. So, get in, and let's go!

> *(He gets in driver's seat.)*

BABE. Tad...?

TAD. *(pouting)* No, I've had enough. I'm not going.

CORKY. Come on, Tad. Let's see if we can make it in time for the reception. It's a challenge.

TAD. No, no, no. Rushing everyplace, then being late, makes me nervous, and gives me a headache and upsets my stomach. I'm not going.

CORKY. Oh, come on, Tad. Don't be a basket case. I'm going.

JINX. Me, too.

BABE. So am I.

TAD. But the car's half mine.

CORKY. I don't care. I'm going anyway. And if I can only take half the car, I'll take my engine.

TAD. What are you talking about?

CORKY. We're going! And if you're *not* going with us, then you need to hold onto your rear end and tail pipe.

TAD. WHAT?! That's crazy! You'll never make it by tomorrow night.

JINX. Sure we will.

CORKY. We'll take turns driving.

BABE. What's the difference?

JINX. Right. Whatever happens, it's new. It's an adventure!

CORKY. All we wanted in the first place was a little romance, adventure and fun. And we've had them all.

JINX. And we'll have more!

BABE. Let's hope so!

JINX. Right! 'Cause, where there's hope, there's life!

CORKY. So, we're off to San Francisco!

BABE. Come on, Tad. For old times sake…romance, adventure, and fun.

> (**BABE** *smiles and nods encouragingly as do the others. Slight pause.* **TAD** *looks reluctant, but finally nods his head.*)

TAD. Okay. O-KAY! One way or another…*San Francisco, here we come*!

BABE. That's the spirit!

CORKY. (*singing from behind the steering wheel*) "Open up that Golden Gate…"

JINX. Oh, I just love happy endings! And, I hope my dad and Sally have a long and happy marriage. Right now I'm so filled with hope, I think I'll explode.

(Just as she looks forward eagerly the rear tire explodes. They all turn slowly and look as the tire hisses. **TAD** *moans and shakes his head,* **CORKY** *and* **BABE** *smile resignedly and shrug, and* **JINX** *chuckles affectionately as the lights fade.)*

End of Act Two

PRODUCTION NOTES

Casting

The usual casting approach for producing groups is "single casting." That is, one person for each role. And because Corky, Tad and Jinx are on stage for the whole play they are probably *single cast.* However, beyond those three there are many other ways to cast this play. And because several of the roles are small, it's even advisable in order to increase the involvement of the cast in the whole production.

Except for Corky, Tad and Jinx, it is possible to *double cast,* i.e. two actors playing the same role in different performances. This includes twice as many people, but for only half of the performances. And, when actors are double cast they don't get as much rehearsal time.

Another option is *cross casting,* of all roles except Corky, Tad and Jinx. Since this whole story has a myth base, and is written in episodic scenes it's also possible for actors to play different characters in different parts of the play with different costumes, make-up, voice and body movement. They would be playing one role or the other each performance. For example, Actor #1 plays Characters A and B at different times. And Actor #2 plays Characters B and A. They rotate. But they are playing at least one role every performance. The challenge of playing two different characters can be more interesting and add to their experience. And, they will learn new ways to do a role from seeing the other person.

Since this play is episodic, and most characters appear only in one scene, it is also possible to have one actor play *multiple roles.* If the producing group has a limited number of actors available to choose from, or there are character actors in the group who like the experience of playing different types of characters, it is possible to have one actor play multiple roles in the same production.

Another possibility for an actor in one role is to *understudy* one of the major roles. This would involve them in other parts of the play as they learn the lines and blocking for the larger role.

These are not the only possibilities. But it is intended that casting of the characters should give both male and female actors a larger challenge, more experience and enhance the spirit and theatricality of the play. Whatever approach is used, casting decisions usually depend on things such as:

1. Physical appearance: age and type of build
2. Psychological believability
3. Acting Ability
4. Availability
5. Needs of the particular producing group
6. Enthusiasm of the actors involved toward amount of time spent, quality of work and attitude toward the production of this play.

Settings

The general staging of this play may be as simple or complex as the size of the stage, technical resources, skilled stagecraft people and budget will allow. While most of the action takes place in and around the car it is possible to construct the basic car and create believable locations with a minimum of effort and expense.

The Car – *"The Wild Goose"*

Even though most of the play is spent in and around the car there is no need to be accurate or expensive in producing any specific type or make of a "real car." But in case it can be done inexpensively or you are able to get a local merchant to loan parts or there are auto mechanics classes at some school and there are technical people available who can put together something on their basic knowledge that looks moderately real, then it might be worth considering that approach. But, ultimately this is just a stage play – not an automobile factory. So, before you commit to a labor intensive and perhaps expensive approach to produce "something" that resembles some "real car," some sort of creatively simple cartoon-like car might be considered.

Start with the base or chassis with a 6-12-inch high platform that is 3-4 feet wide, and 8-10 long. Put two benches on it, placed as the front seat and the back seat. Make the back seat slightly higher to avoid masking. If desired, foam rubber pads can be cut to fit the benches with an attractive cloth "seat cover" stapled over it. For the engine in front, a large cardboard box or cut cardboard, using tri-wall (three layered cardboard) can be used or a wooden construction. Because the actors need to be seen, it should be a convertible. Doors are not really necessary, and actors and audience could enjoy having the doors pantomimed.

The steering wheel may be real or a pizza tin or round serving tray that is screwed or nailed onto a 2 X 2 board that goes into "the engine" and is fastened to the base platform with angle irons. The wheels can also be painted pizza tins or cheap circular trays or painted circular cardboard cutouts. With a hole in the center they can be fastened to cardboard with a paper fastener or using a screw or nut and bolt can be attached to the engine if it is wood.

The headlights can be shiny aluminum pie tins and attached to the "engine" in the same way that the wheels are. "Wild Goose" can be painted someplace on the side. In addition, paint or personalize the design in whatever way would be creative. This all may be capped off with some kind of ornamental or decorative radiator cap. (See drawings of a simple car at the end of these Production Notes.)

In deciding where to locate the car, and the different settings, the major consideration should probably be on the basis of the size of the stage space in which it is to be performed. If it is a relatively small stage – roughly 18' to 26' proscenium opening – then putting the car on one side and all the other settings on the other would seem to be a feasible answer.

If the proscenium opening is approximately 28' to 36' or more, then it is suggested that the car be located in the center of the stage with other scenes stage right and left. If possible, this is a better solution since so much of the action takes place in the car. Another possibility is to put the car in the center and locate the other scenes, if there is space, on the apron in front of the proscenium.

Background

A sky blue cyclorama in the background behind the car can enhance the feeling of outdoors. If the stage is large enough and deep enough, it is possible to enhance the visual effect with rolling blackboards covered with painted scenery that could represent passing landscapes or commercial billboards with products that come from California. Rolling blackboards turned around may also be used for displaying general and specific signs behind the scenes. (See "Signs" in Production Notes.)

Settings – Other Than The Car.

A breakdown of time spent in an area can be a guideline to the amount of time and space spent on settings other than the car. All scenes are defined by character's lines and specific signs. Other scenes involve:

- House in Sausalito at night, 2 pages. Since Corky is in a spotlight on the telephone nothing special is required.
- Carnival Concession on Santa Cruz Boardwalk morning, 6 pages. This needs a feeling of a carnival-like atmosphere. There is a booth with signs, counter with balls, table in corner with prizes. And stool by counter.
- Interior of Swan Café and Post Office, 7 pages. This needs a feeling of small rural restaurant. There is a large posted menu on the wall. There is a counter with napkin holders and salt and pepper shakers, small table in corner with checkered tablecloth and two chairs on side.
- Margo's Mobile home, 5 pages. This needs a feeling of a home of an "old actress" of the past who is now earning money by telling fortunes. The counter is upstage as a shelf with flowers and a bell, a small table in the center with a lace tablecloth and fortune teller's crystal ball and chairs on either side. There is a sign that says she is a Fortune Teller.
- Desert Oasis and Gas Station in Borrego Springs, 1 page. This has a small counter in a brief space and only needs to be indicated by a sign.
- Gaslight District of San Diego, 17 pages. This involves the whole stage including the car and a sign on a building.

Construction Considerations for Settings

These locations may be defined by:

1. Signs and basic furniture and set pieces and props placed on an open floor. Or,

2. They may be further defined by putting the settings on a 6" platform to establish a specific area such as Swan Café or Margo's Mobile Home. Or,

3. They may be even further defined by a frame or a low wall or high wall at the back of what would become a unit set.

Unit Set

A basic set that is the same for many settings but can be changed to look different through the rearrangement of the furniture, set pieces, props and signs to indicate and define different locations. The unit set includes a 6-inch platform, approximately 8 feet by 12 feet. It may have just a frame outline of wall. Or, the back wall along the 12-foot side of the platform with wood paneling that has a curtained doorway on the left end. Or there may be a full-length wall with a doorway suggested on the side. And there are two side flats coming forward for about two feet for support. Unit sets are not necessary to achieve the effect of the locale. But if there is space and they are used they may enhance a specific setting. Or they may be modified and simplified for your stage and production, depending on size of stage, technical resources, skilled stagecraft people and budget. (See drawings at end for visual suggestions.)

Furniture and Set Pieces

The same type set pieces or furniture are used in most of the settings with different arrangements. What makes each setting appear different is a rearrangement of the basic set pieces, the changing of the décor and the general and specific signs that define each location.

These are basic items that help to define each location
1. One 4 – foot long counter or shelf.
2. There is one stool that is adjacent to the counter.
3. A small round table
4. There are 2 chairs.
5. Signs: menus, posters and pictures are hung appropriately for each setting.

Note: If the car is in the center and the short scenes are on both sides of the stage, some of the furniture and set props may need to be duplicated or find a way to put the items on the other side of the stage without breaking the flow of the action.

Signs

The painted signs that designate locations are an important part of enhancing each setting. Each sign may be painted in a distinctive style for the location. Depending on the theatre and the production there are many ways to display these signs. They may be hung:
1. On the back wall of a unit set.
2. On the back wall of a small theatre.
3. On the side of a tall ladder.
4. On a tall flat support by a triangular brace.
5. On a one side of a rolling blackboard mentioned in "background."
6. On a batten
7. On a peraktoi. A peraktoi is a three-sided prism – that is used like a kiosk. It is made of narrow flats or jogs or heavy cardboard and turns to define each new general location. It is possible to change these signs as well as turn the prism.

Hand Props & Set Dressings and Decor

These are the properties used by individual actors in each scene and items used for set decoration.

Opening Scenes – in House and Car

Cell phone – Corky
Small duffle bag and backpack or small suitcase, assorted traveling materials – Corky and Tad
Map and camera (or facsimile) – Corky
Light weight blanket (not seen until later) Tad and Jinx
Colorful embroidered handbag with notepad and pencils – Jinx

Concession Booth at Santa Cruz Boardwalk

Sign on wall: "Game of Life / Take a Chance"
Tennis balls on counter – (to be used to hit the target on wall)
Fuzzy animals and balloons for prizes on table in corner
Teddy Bear – Corky.

Swan Café and Post Office

Sign on wall: "Menu for Today"
Checkered tablecloth on round table
Napkin holder, salt and pepper on counter
Mail – Uncle Herman
Stormy's Treasure Box – Herman gives to Tad
(The Treasure Box can have "evil figures" made of rubber and plastic toys)
Bag of food and snacks – Lita gives to Corky.

Parked Outside San Luis Obispo

Bag of fresh fruit – Corky

In Car on Way to Los Angeles

Light weight blanket – packed earlier, but seen here – Tad and Jinx

In Margo's Mobile Home in Santa Monica

Sign on wall: "Madame Margo – Fortune Teller"
Lace tablecloth on round table
Crystal ball on round table (optional)
Bowl of flowers on shelf in corner (optional)
Dinner Bell on shelf (optional) – Jinx

In Desert Area

Towel on head – Corky
Bag of bagels and raisins – Religious Person
Key in car – Religious Person
Handgun – Religious Person
Money in wallets – Corky and Tad
Jewelry – Jinx
Coin purse – Religious Person
Postcard from Stormy – Spit Partch to Jinx
Harmonica (Optional) Spit Partch

Items in Treasure Box: Rodeo flyer, belt buckle, turquoise ring, silver spur - Jinx and Corky
Gas can – Tad

Street Scene in Gaslight area of San Diego
Sing on wall: "Murphy's OK Feed Store
Cowboy hat and gun and bag of money – Stormy
Gun – Villain

Sound & Sound Person
It is possible to have all sounds recorded and played from the control booth. However, in order to suggest and enhance the presentational or theatrical aspects of the play, a Sound Person can be cast and located in a visible location on stage at down right or on the apron in front of proscenium.

The primary sounds are connected with The Car and include: car starting, taking off, lurching, picking up in speed, slowing down, screeching of tires and stopping. These all may be done orally to add to spirit of the play.

In addition to the car sounds, the most needed sound is what is called "Time/Travel Music." The Time/Travel sounds need to have the musical sound and feeling of a car traveling on a highway and time is passing. These should be a brief series of chords for transition. This may be created by a guitar or possibly harmonica or other available instruments.

A guitar may also be used to produce magical qualities of the Treasure Box with harp-like sounds. The musical sounds for time/travel and the Treasure Box harp sounds may be performed by the same person that does the car sounds. Or, they could be done by another Sound Person with an instrument.

Other sounds might include: seagulls, foghorns, and dogs barking in distance (all optional), distant carnival sounds, bell from bell tower in distance: Bong, Bong, Clang! and Harp Chords, dinner bell (optional), Gong, mood setting music for hot dreary desert, harmonica (optional), Gunshots (clipboard snapping metal on wood, and Tire exploding and Hissing.

Sound, Act I
    (Optional) Seagulls, Fog Horns (kazoo or hum into mashed potato container) and Dogs barking (oral)
    Engine turns over, but doesn't start
    Engine starts
    TAD guns motor and takes off with a lurch.
        TIME TRAVEL MUSIC – Guitar or Harmonica
    Increase motor speed
    Screeches of tires – Screeching to Stop.
    TAD accelerates car
    Motor decelerating and stopping
        DISTANT CARNIVAL SOUNDS
        TIME TRAVEL MUSIC

Squealing tires for swerving and screeching tires for stopping
TAD starts engine
>   TIME TRAVEL MUSIC
Tires screeching to a stop and Tad turns off motor
Bell from bell Tower – BONG, BONG, CLANG! (Metal stroked on wine glass)
CORKY starts the engine and accelerates.
>   TIME TRAVEL MUSIC
>   HARP CHORDS
Car decelerates and stops
(Optional) Dinner bell – on set (or short soft strokes on wine glass) and
>   GONG (metal on mashed potato container)

Sound, Act II
>   (Optional) Drum roll and or bass drum and/or
>   OMINOUS MUSIC CHORDS to capture hot desert morning
Brakes screeching. Engine stops
>   HARMONICA / Car starting rapidly
>   TIME TRAVEL MUSIC
Car begins to chug, sputter and lurch to a jerky stop
>   HARP CHORDS (or facsimile) 3 times
>   HARP CHORDS – Tremulous
>   HARP CHORDS
>   HARP CHORDS
>   HARP CHORDS   - "Spacey sound – unearthly"
>   HARP CHORDS – Going wild – then fading
TAD starts motor and takes off
>   TIME TRAVEL MUSIC
Gunshots # 1, # 2, # 3 (snapping clip on clipboard)
Gunshots # 4
Gunshots # 5 and # 6
Tires explodes (Thud on mashed potato container) and Tire hisses (oral)

Lights

There are two or three areas depending on number of playing areas where the action takes place. When the scenes are in the car the rest of the stage is dark or in a half-light. The whole stage is lighted in the last scene in the Gaslight District. Lights from each area may overlap to allow each playing area to be larger.

Color media could match weather conditions: cool (blues) on the coast in Act One. And in Act Two, hot (pink and yellow gold) for the desert scenes. Or, since the sky is not even blue – it is white – it is possible to use "gel-less" light. There is a green light on Corky and Jinx when they open the Treasure Box and release all the sins. The movie-making scene in the Gaslight District that takes place on the whole stage and possibly in the audience area. This wider area might call for extra lighting.

Costume

It is a modern play and the costumes are modern. Corky wears bright clothes and a floppy tennis hat with sea and sky blue the predominant color. Tad wears western, desert type clothes with brown and green as the major colors. Jinx wears slightly crazy and outlandish clothes that are accented by scarves and jewelry. The other characters should be costumed according to their personality and profession.

(See Character Descriptions.)

THE CAR

"THE WILD GOOSE"

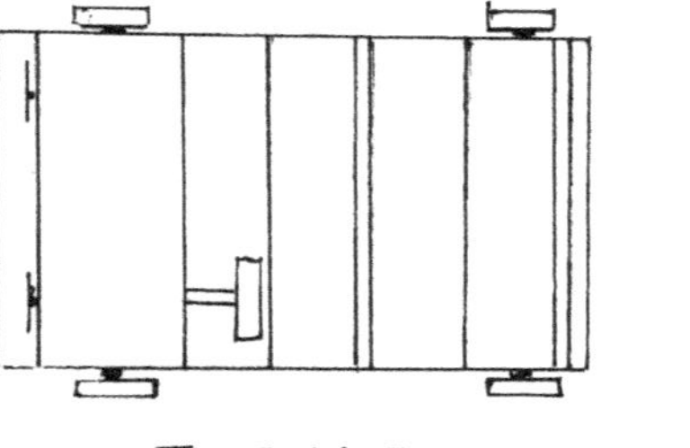

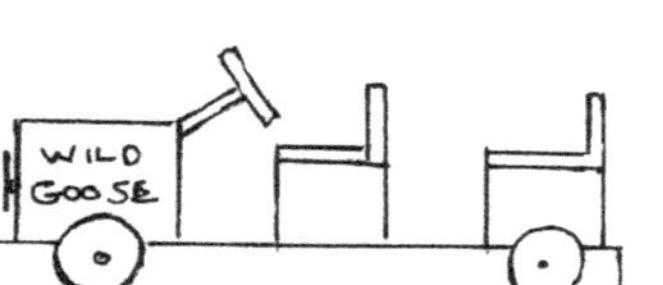

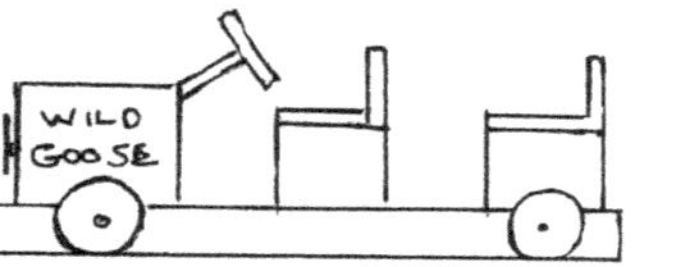

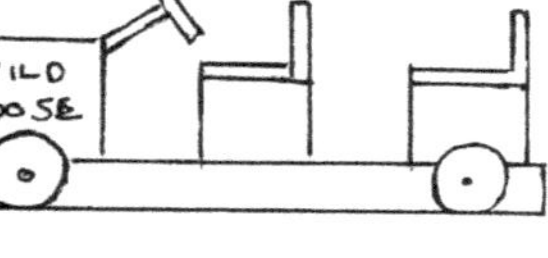

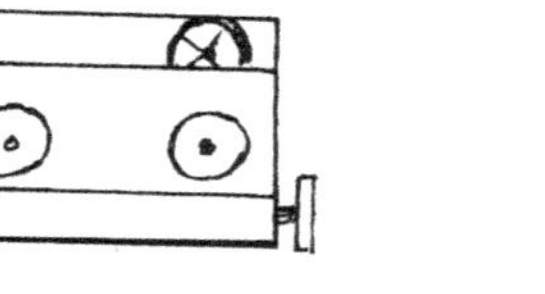

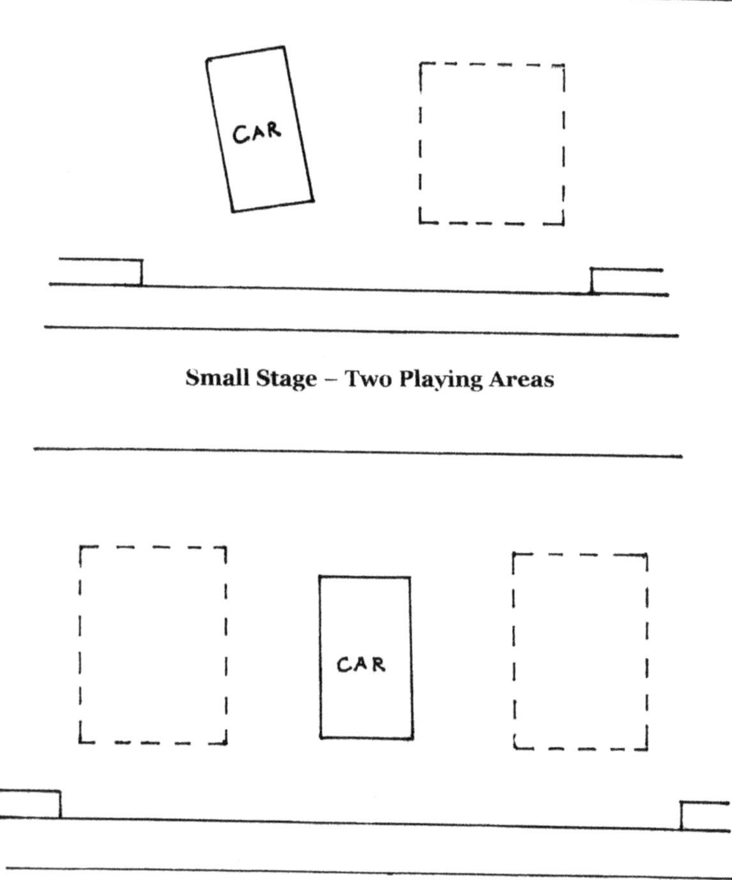

Small Stage – Two Playing Areas

LARGE STAGE – Three Playing Areas

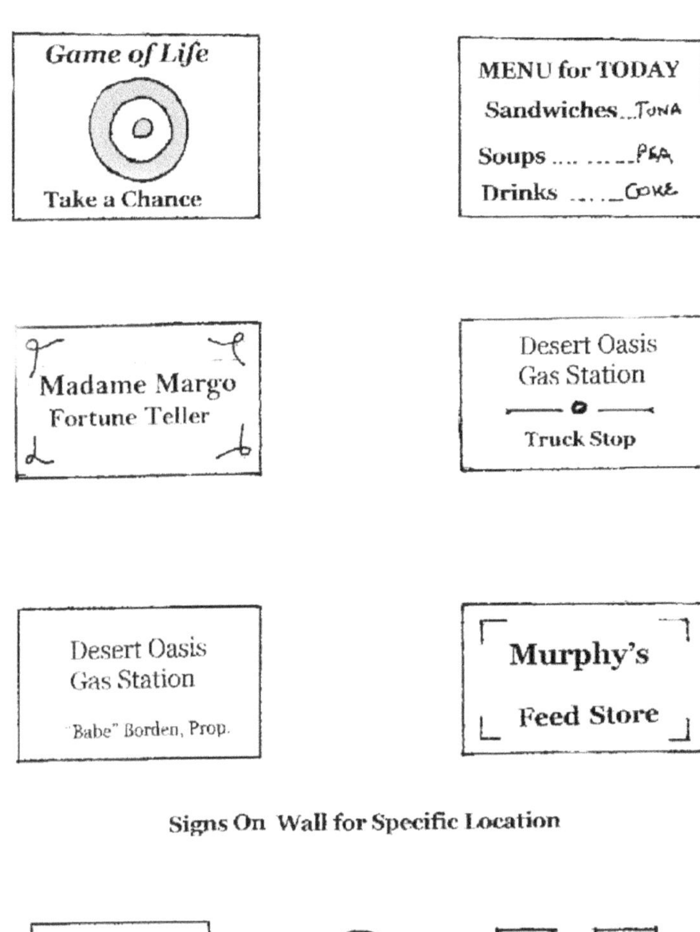

Signs On Wall for Specific Location

Furniture & Set Pieces

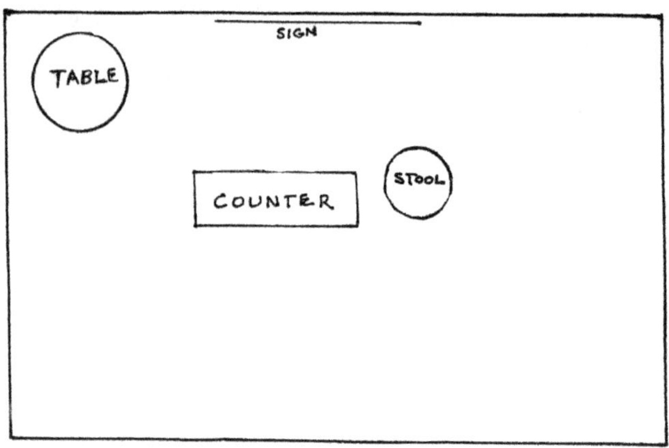

Concession Booth on The Boardwalk

Swan Café and Post Office

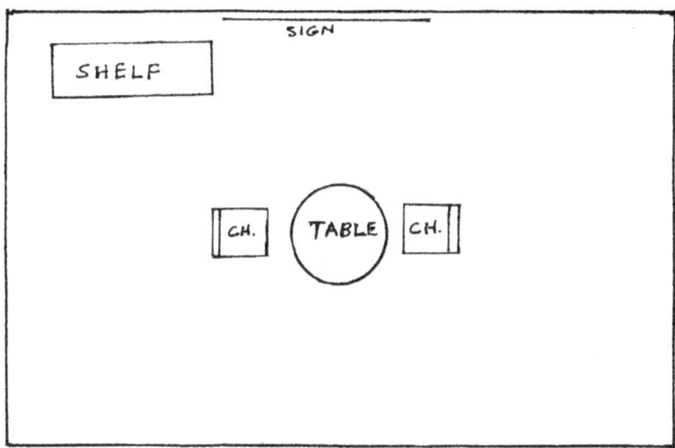

Margo's Mobile Home

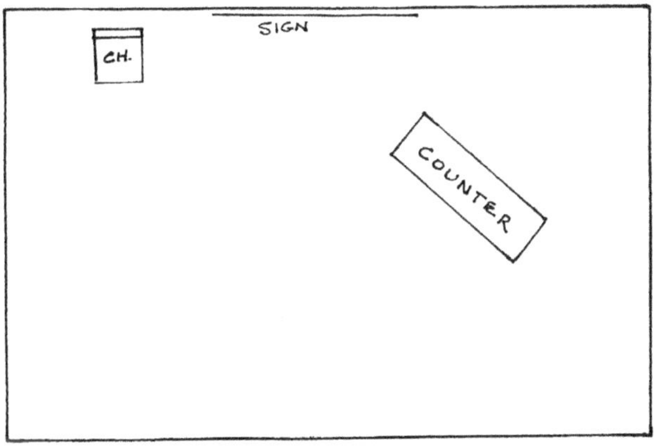

Desert Oasis Gas Station

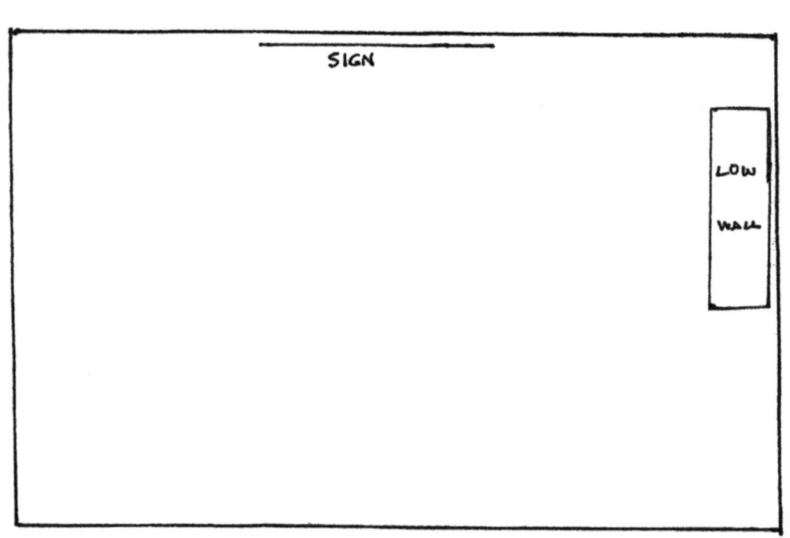

Street Scene in Gaslight District

* 9 7 8 0 8 7 4 4 0 2 2 5 4 *